The Heretic of Soana

The Heretic of Soana

Gerhart Hauptmann

Translated by Bayard Quincy Morgan

CALDER

CALDER PUBLICATIONS
an imprint of

ALMA BOOKS LTD
3 Castle Yard
Richmond
Surrey TW10 6TF
United Kingdom
www.calderpublications.com

The Heretic of Soana first published in German as *Der Ketzer von Soana* in 1918. First published in this translation by John Calder (Publishers) Ltd in 1960
This revised edition first published by Calder Publications in 2020

Translation © Bayard Quincy Morgan, 1960, 2020

Cover design by Will Dady

Printed in Great Britain by CPI Group (UK) Ltd, Croydon CR0 4YY

ISBN: 978-0-7145-4968-2

All rights reserved. No part of this publication may be reproduced, stored in or introduced into a retrieval system, or transmitted, in any form or by any means (electronic, mechanical, photocopying, recording or otherwise), without the prior written permission of the publisher. This book is sold subject to the condition that it shall not be resold, lent, hired out or otherwise circulated without the express prior consent of the publisher.

Contents

Introduction   VII

The Heretic of Soana
   The Heretic of Soana   I
   Notes   113

Introduction

Gerhart Hauptmann was born on 15th November 1862 at Ober Salzbrunn in Silesia, where his father owned a small hotel. Even as a child Gerhart showed signs of an exceptional personality, being content with his own company and thoughts rather than participating with his brothers and other children in the normal pursuits of youth. There was no school at the little spa town, so he was sent to a grammar school at Breslau – where he was not a particularly brilliant scholar – and he made no great success of orthodox education. His father, in the hopes of finding the right career for him, placed him on an uncle's farm to learn agriculture, but after two years it was obvious that his exploring mind could not find satisfaction in farm work. Gerhart returned to Breslau, hoping to find more congenial study by attending an art school – but again, this was not a success. From there, he went to Jena for a year, and became a student at the university. He heard lectures in science, history and philosophy from, among others, such well-known philosophers as Haeckel and Eucken. Following these studies, he travelled extensively through Switzerland, Spain and Italy, and eventually established himself as a sculptor in Rome. A severe illness, however, forced him to give up this career, and in 1884 he returned home to Germany. After staying a few months in Dresden, he finally settled in Berlin in 1885, bringing with him his young wife, the sister-in-law of one of his brothers.

The period of irresolution and unsteadiness was now at an end. Hauptmann met the members of the *"Freie Bühne"*

("Free Stage"), an association of young writers and poets in Berlin, and suddenly recognized his vocation to be a writer.

He wrote his first drama in 1889, *Vor Sonnenaufgang* (*Before Dawn*), a literary achievement of the highest significance in its pioneering movement towards realism; its first performance caused a theatrical scandal, but it was immediately acclaimed as a masterpiece, and Hauptmann's name was made famous all over Germany. In 1892, there followed *Die Weber* (*The Weavers*), which was an even greater success, and indeed was a milestone in German literary history. Here, for the first time, the suffering masses act as the hero of a play. The bourgeois audience was shocked.

Hauptmann's fame is based on his dramatic work. After *Die Weber* there followed *Kollege Crampton* (*Colleague Krampton*, 1892), *Der Biberpelz* (*The Beaver Coat*, 1893), *Florian Geyer* (1896), *Fuhrmann Henschel* (*Carter Henschel*, 1898), *Michael Kramer* (1900), *Der rote Hahn* (*The Conflagration*, 1901), *Rose Bernd* (1903), *Elga* (1905), *Die Jungfern vom Bischofsberg* (*The Maidens of the Mount*, 1908) and *Die Ratten* (*The Rats*, 1911). The dramas have not lost their appeal to present-day audiences, and are still produced – not only in German theatres, but on other European stages. It was chiefly for these plays that Gerhart Hauptmann received the Nobel Prize in Literature in 1912.

Although Hauptmann is considered one of the greatest exponents of Naturalism in German literature, choosing as his themes the joys, sorrows and even the ugliness of everyday life among the common people, many of his writings would also classify him as a Romantic. Among his early dramas were dream visions such as *Hanneles Himmelfahrt* (*The Ascension of Little Hanele*, 1895), fairy tales like *Die versunkene Glocke* (*The Sunken Bell*, 1896) and *Und Pippa tanzt* (*And Pippa Dances*, 1906), as well as folk tales and sagas, such as *Der arme Heinrich* (*Henry of Auë*, 1902), *Der weisse Heiland* (*The White Saviour*, 1908), *Griselda* (1909) and *Indipohdi* (1920).

In *Dorothea Angermann* (1926) and *Vor Sonnenuntergang* (*Before Sunset*, 1932) Hauptmann reverted to his theme of the suffering of the lower classes. As he grew older, he became attracted to demonic subjects, such as those he found in the old Greek sagas of the Atrides, and between 1941 and 1943 he wrote *Iphigenie in Delphi, Agamemnons Tod* (*The Death of Agamemnon*), *Elektra* and *Iphigenie in Aulis*.

There is scarcely an artistic subject which he did not include in his writings, and he used almost every literary form – the drama, the novel, the novella, the short story and poetry. In the novella form, *Der Ketzer von Soana* (*The Heretic of Soana*) is a masterpiece of extraordinary beauty.

Although his literary fame was universally acclaimed and his plays were included in the repertoires of all the more important theatres in Germany, towards the end of his days Hauptmann lived a quiet and modest life in Agnetendorf, a small town in the beautiful Riesengebirge in Silesia, where he had settled in 1891. There he stayed with short interruptions until the end of his life. The Hitler regime brought no alteration to his way of life – as an old man he was fully immersed in his work. Real tragedy came when, in 1945, the Poles occupied his beloved homeland. He witnessed millions of his fellow countrymen being driven away from their homesteads, forced westwards as refugees; he was one of the few allowed to stay on alone in Agnetendorf, to await his death, which occurred the following year, in 1946.

The Heretic of Soana

TRAVELLERS CAN SET OUT for the summit of Monte Generoso from Mendrisio, or by the funicular from Capolago, or from Melide via Soana, where the road is most arduous. The entire district belongs to Ticino, a Swiss canton of Italian population.

At a great height, mountain climbers not infrequently came upon the figure of a bespectacled goatherd, whose exterior was striking in still other respects. The face indicated a man of education, despite the tanned skin. He looked not unlike the bronze statue of John the Baptist by Donatello in the cathedral at Siena. His hair was dark and fell in curls over his brown shoulders. His clothing consisted of goatskin.

When a troop of strangers approached this man, the guides usually began to laugh. Then, when the tourists saw him, they often burst out into unmannerly guffaws, or made provocative remarks; they felt justified by the strangeness of the sight. The herdsman paid no attention to them. He did not even turn his head.

All the guides really seemed to be on good terms with him. Often they would clamber up to him and have long confidential talks with him. When they returned and were asked by the tourists what sort of strange saint he was, they would usually observe a mysterious silence until he was out of earshot. But those travellers whose curiosity was still active would then find that this person had an obscure history and, popularly called the "heretic of Soana", enjoyed a dubious reputation, mingled with superstitious fear.

When the writer of these pages was still young in years and often had the good fortune to spend glorious weeks in beautiful Soana, it was inevitable that he should ascend Generoso now and then, and that he too should catch a glimpse one day of the so-called heretic of Soana. He did not forget the man's appearance. And after he had collected all sorts of contradictory information about him, there ripened within him the resolve to see him again – indeed, to make him an actual visit.

The writer was strengthened in his purpose by a German Swiss, the physician of Soana, who assured him that the eccentric fellow was not averse to receiving visits from educated persons. He himself had once called on him. "I really ought to be angry with him," said he, "because the fellow encroaches on my preserves. But he lives so high up, so far away, and is only consulted – thank Heaven – in secret by those few who would not object to being cured by the Devil." The physician continued, "You must know that the people believe he had sold himself to the Devil – a view which is not contested by the clergy, because they originated it. In the beginning, they say, the man fell a prey to an evil spell, until he himself became a confirmed villain and a hellish sorcerer. As for me, I did not notice that he had either talons or horns on him."

Of his visits to this strange person the writer still has an exact recollection. The manner of the first meeting was remarkable. A special circumstance gave it the character of an accident, for the visitor found himself by a steep wayside, face to face with a helpless mother goat which had just dropped one kid and was about to give birth to a second. The lonely creature in her distress, looking fearlessly at him as if she had expected his help, and the deep mystery of any sort of birth there, amid the tremendous rocky wilds, made the profoundest impression upon him. But he hastened his steps, for he concluded that this animal must belong to the herd of the eccentric, and wished to summon him to help. He encountered him among his goats and cattle, told him what he had observed and led him to the labouring mother, behind which the second little kid, damp and covered with blood, was already lying in the grass.

With the assurance of a physician, with the tender love of the compassionate Samaritan, the animal was now cared for by its owner. After he had waited a certain time, he took one of the newborn kids under each arm and set out slowly, followed by the mother, her heavy udder almost scraping the ground, on the way to his dwelling. The visitor was not only favoured with the friendliest thanks, but invited in the most cordial manner to accompany the herdsman.

The hermit had erected several buildings on the Alp, which he owned. One of them resembled outwardly a rude heap of stones. Inside it contained warm, dry stabling. The goat and her kids were stabled here, while the visitor was conducted higher up the mountain to a square whitewashed hut which, leaning against the wall of Generoso, stood on a vine-covered terrace. Not far from the little gate there shot out of the mountain a stream of water as thick as your arm, filling an immense stone basin that had been hewn out of the rock. Beside this basin, an iron-bound door opened into a mountain cave, which soon turned out to be a vaulted cellar.

One had from this spot – which, when viewed from the valley, seemed to hang at an inaccessible height – a glorious view, of which, however, the author does not intend to speak. On that occasion, to be sure, when he enjoyed it for the first time, he passed from speechless astonishment to loud exclamation of rapture and back again to speechless astonishment. His host, however, who just at this moment stepped out into the open again from the dwelling, where he had been looking for something, seemed all at once to be walking with quieter feet. The way he acted – indeed, the entire calm, tranquil bearing of his friendly host – the visitor did not allow to escape him. It served him as an admonition to be sparing of words, chary of questions. He was already too fond of the strange herdsman to run the risk of alienating him by even a hint of curiosity or obtrusiveness.

The visitor of that day can still see standing on the terrace the round stone table, with its circle of benches. He sees it covered with all the good things which the heretic of Soana spread out upon it: the most glorious Stracchino di Lecco,* delicious Italian wheat bread, salami sausage, olives, figs and medlars, and then a jug of red wine, which he had drawn fresh from the grotto. When they sat down, the long-haired, bearded host, with his goatskin garments, looked warmly into the visitor's eyes, and at the same time clasped his right hand, as if wishing to intimate an affection for him.

Of what was said at this first meeting the writer remembers only a little. The mountain herdsman wished to be called Ludovico. He related some things about Argentina. Once, when the tinkle of the Angelus* came up from far below, he made a remark about this "certainly provoking noise". The name of Seneca was mentioned. There was also some superficial talk about Swiss politics. Finally, the host wished to know a number of things about Germany, because it was the visitor's home. When the visitor was ready to leave, the hermit said, "You will always be welcome here."

Although the writer of these pages, as he will not conceal, was avid to hear the history of this man, even on his renewed visits he avoided betraying any interest in it. People had communicated to him a few external facts in conversations which he had had in Soana – facts which were said to be the cause for Ludovico's being described as the heretic of Soana – but he took far more interest in finding out in what sense this appellation was correct, and in what peculiar inward vicissitudes – what special philosophy – the form of Ludovico's life had its roots. Yet he reserved his questions, and was richly rewarded for it.

He usually found Ludovico alone, either among the animals of his herds or in his cell. A few times he came upon him as he, like Crusoe, was milking the goats with his own hand or was putting the kids to a recalcitrant mother. Then he seemed wholly absorbed in the herdsman's calling: he rejoiced over the female that dragged her swelling udder on the ground, over the male when he was in heat and mating. Of one he would say, "Does he not look like the Evil One himself? Just see his eyes. What power, what sparkling rage, fury, maliciousness! And, at the same time, what sacred fire!" But to the author it seemed as if the eyes of the speaker held the same devilish flame as that which he had called a sacred fire. His smile would take on a rigid and fierce character; he would show his splendid white teeth and at the same time fall into a state of dreaming as he observed with the glance of the expert one of his demoniacal matadors at his useful labour.

Sometimes the heretic played the pan pipe, and the visitor would hear its simple scales as he drew near. On such an occasion the conversation naturally turned to music, and the herdsman unfolded strange views. Never, when he was among his flocks, did Ludovico speak of anything but the animals and their habits, of the herdsman's calling and its usages. Not uncommonly would he pursue the psychology of the animals, the mode of life of the herders, back into the remotest past, thus betraying a knowledge of no common scope. He was speaking of Apollo, telling how the latter tended the herds of Laomedon and Admetus, and was a servant and herdsman. "I should like to know with what instrument he used to make music for his flocks." And as if he were speaking of something real, he finished: "By Heaven, I should have liked to listen to him." Those were the moments when the shaggy recluse might perhaps cause one to suspect that his powers of understanding were not quite undamaged. On the other hand, the idea gained a certain justification when he proved in how many ways a flock may be influenced and guided by music. With one note he chased them to their feet, with others he calmed them down. With certain notes he brought them from afar, with others he induced the animals to scatter or to trail along behind him, close at his heels.

There were also visits when almost nothing was said. Once, when the oppressive heat of a June afternoon had ascended even to the pastures of Generoso, Ludovico, surrounded by his recumbent, cud-chewing flocks, was found likewise outstretched in a state of blissful somnolence. He only blinked at the visitor and motioned to him to stretch out in the grass likewise. Then, after this had been done and both had lain a while in silence, he suddenly began in a trailing voice:

"You know that Eros is older than Kronos – and mightier, too! Do you feel this silent glow about us? Eros! Do you hear how the cricket is chirping? Eros!" At this moment two lizards, chasing each other, darted like a flash across him as he lay there. He repeated, "Eros, Eros!" – and, as if he had given the command for it, two strong bucks now arose and attacked each other with their curved horns. He left them undisturbed, although the combat grew more and more heated. The clash of the blows rang louder and louder, and more and more frequent. And again he said, "Eros, Eros!"

And now there came to the ears of the visitor, for the first time, words that made him particularly attentive, because they shed – or, at least, seemed to shed – some light on the question of why Ludovico was called "the heretic" by the people. "I would rather," he said, "worship a live he-goat or a live bull than a hanged man on a gallows. I do not live in an age that does that. I hate – I abhor it. Jupiter Ammon was represented with ram's horns. Pan has the leg of a goat, Bacchus the horns of a bull. I mean the Bacchus Tauriformis or Tauricornis of the Romans. Mithra, the sun god, is represented as a bull. All peoples used to revere the bull, the he-goat, the ram, and to shed their sacred blood in sacrifice. To that I say: amen! For the procreative power is the creative power – procreation and creation are the same thing. To be sure, the cult of that power is no tepid whimpering of monks and nuns. Once I dreamt of Sita, the wife of Vishnu, who assumed human form under the name of Rama. The priests died in her embrace. Then for a moment I had a glimpse of all sorts of mysteries – of the mystery of the black procreation in the green grass, of the mother-of-pearl-coloured lust, of ecstasies and torpors, of the secret of the yellow maize kernels, of all fruits, all swellings, all colours of every kind. I could have bellowed in a frenzy of pain when I caught sight of the pitiless, all-powerful Sita. I thought I should die of desire."

During this revelation, the writer of these lines felt like an involuntary eavesdropper. He arose with a few words that were meant to give the impression that he had not heard the monologue, but had been preoccupied with other matters. He started to leave. Ludovico would not permit it. And so the visitor was entertained again on the mountain terrace, and what happened this time was significant and unforgettable.

Directly upon his arrival the visitor was ushered into the dwelling, the interior of the hut which has already been described. It was square, neat, had a fireplace and resembled the simple study of a scholar. It contained ink, pen, paper and a small library – principally of Greek and Latin authors. "Why should I conceal from you," said the herdsman, "that I am of a good family, and that I had a misguided youth and a good education? You will, of course, wish to know how I turned from an unnatural person into a natural one, from a captive into a freeman, from a warped and morose man into a happy and contented one? Or how I shut myself out of society and Christianity?" He laughed loudly. "Perhaps I shall write some day the story of my conversion." The visitor, whose suspense had reached a climax, once more found himself suddenly driven far from the goal. Nor did he progress much when his host wound up by declaring that the cause of his rebirth was this: he worshipped natural symbols.

In the shade of the rock, on the terrace, by the brim of the overflowing basin, in delicious coolness, they supped more richly than the first time: smoked ham, cheese and wheat bread, figs, fresh medlars and wine. They chatted about many things – not boisterously, but with quiet gaiety. But now there came a moment which is as present to the writer as if it had just passed.

The bronzed herdsman gave an impression of savagery with the long, unkempt curls of his hair and beard and his goatskin clothing. He has been compared to Donatello's John the Baptist. And indeed, his face and the features of that John had much similarity in the fineness of the lines. Ludovico was really handsome, on closer inspection – provided one could set aside the distorting eyeglasses. On the other hand, to be sure, it was through them that the entire figure gained, aside from a slightly comic effect, its puzzlingly strange and arresting character. At the moment of which we are speaking, the entire person underwent an alteration. Since the bronze-like aspect of his body had also found expression in a certain rigidness of the features, it disappeared as they became animated and rejuvenated. He smiled, one might say, in an access of boyish embarrassment. "What I am going to ask you now," said he, "I have not yet proposed to any man. Where I have suddenly found the courage I really don't know myself. From the old habit of past days I still read occasionally, and still handle pen and ink, too. So I have written down in idle winter hours a plain story of events which are said to have taken place here, in and about Soana, long before my time. You will find it extremely simple, but it attracted me for all sorts of reasons, which I will not discuss now. Tell me briefly and frankly: will you go into the house with me once more, and do you feel inclined to waste some of your time in hearing this story, which has cost me too many a profitless hour? I should rather dissuade than urge you. Moreover, if you say so, I will take the pages of my manuscript even now and throw them down into the abyss."

Of course this did not happen. He took the jug of wine, went into the house with the visitor, and the two sat facing each other. The mountain herdsman had unrolled from the finest goat's leather a manuscript written in a monkish hand on strong paper. As if to give himself courage, he drank the visitor's health once more before pushing off from the shore, as it were, to plunge into the stream of the narrative, and then began in a melodious voice.

THE NARRATIVE OF
THE MOUNTAIN HERDSMAN

On a mountain slope above the Lake of Lugano there is to be found, among many others, a little nest in the mountains, which one can reach from the shore of the lake by a steep, winding mountain road in about an hour. The houses of the village – which, like those in most of the Italian places of that region, consist of a jumbled grey ruin made of stone and mortar – turn their fronts towards a gorge-like valley, which is formed by the meadows and terraces of the hamlet, and on the other side by an immense slope of the over-towering mountain-giant, Monte Generoso.

Into this valley, and at the very spot where it really comes to an end as a narrow gorge, a waterfall pours down from a valley that lies perhaps a hundred yards higher. Its roar, varying with the time of the day and the year, and with the prevailing currents of the air, whether strong or weak, supplies the hamlet with continual music.

Into this parish, a long time ago, there was transferred a priest of about five-and-twenty, whose name was Raffaele Francesco. He had been born in Ligornetto, hence in Ticino, and could boast of being a member of the same family, long resident there, which had produced the greatest sculptor of united Italy – who was likewise born in Ligornetto and finally died there, too.*

The young priest had spent his childhood with relatives in Milan, and had been educated at various seminaries of

Switzerland and Italy. From his mother, who was of noble stock, he derived the serious trend of his character, which impelled him at an early age and without any vacillation into the arms of a religious calling.

Francesco, who always wore glasses, made himself conspicuous in the company of his fellow pupils by exemplary industry, strict living and piety. Even his mother was obliged to suggest to him delicately that as a future secular priest he might well indulge in a little pleasure, and that he was not really bound by the strictest monastic rules. As soon as he had been ordained, however, it was his sole desire to find a parish as remote as possible, where as a sort of hermit he could consecrate himself unreservedly, and more than even before, to the service of God, his Son and the Holy Mother.

Now, when he had come to the little hamlet of Soana and had taken possession of the parsonage, which was built onto the church, the mountain dwellers soon observed that he was of a totally different stamp from his predecessor – even in appearance, for the latter had been a massive, bull-like peasant, who kept the pretty women and girls of the place under his control with the aid of wholly other means than ecclesiastical penances and penalties. Francesco, on the other hand, was pale and delicate. His eyes were deep-set. Hectic spots glowed on the clouded skin over his cheekbones. Then too there were his glasses, to this day in the eyes of simple folk a symbol of preceptorial severity and learning. At first the wives and daughters of the village had resisted him somewhat, but after the lapse of four or five weeks, he too had got them into his power after his own fashion, and to a greater extent, in fact, than the other priest.

As soon as Francesco stepped out into the street through the little door of the tiny parsonage nestling up against the church, he would have children and women thronging about him, kissing his hand with true veneration. And the number of times in the day he was called to the confessional by the little bell on the church mounted up so by evening that his newly appointed housekeeper, who was nearly seventy years old, would exclaim that she had never known before how many angels were concealed in the otherwise rather corrupt village of Soana. In short, the name of the young pastor, Francesco Vela, spread far and wide through the countryside, and he very soon came to be reputed a saint.

Francesco did not allow himself to be disturbed by all this, and was far from cultivating within himself any other consciousness than that he was tolerably fulfilling his duties. He said his masses, performed with unabated zeal all the churchly rites of divine service, and – for the little schoolroom was in the parsonage – attended besides to the duties of secular instruction.

One evening at the beginning of March, there was a very violent pull at the bell of the little parsonage, and when the housekeeper came to open the door and threw the light of her lantern out into the dismal weather, there stood before the door a somewhat uncouth fellow who wished to see the pastor. After she had closed the door again, the crone betook herself to her young master's room and announced, not without noticeable anxiety, that there was a visitor at this late hour. But Francesco, who had made it one of his duties not to turn away anyone that needed him, whoever it might be, merely said shortly, looking up from the pages of some church father, "Go, Petronilla, show him in."

Soon afterwards there stood before the pastor's table a man of about forty, whose outward appearance was that of the peasants of that region, only far more neglected – indeed wholly uncared for. He was barefoot. Ragged, rain-soaked trousers were held up by a strap above the hips. His shirt was open. The brown, hairy breast led to a shaggy throat and a face densely overgrown with black hair and whiskers, in the midst of which flamed two darkly glowing eyes.

The man had thrown, shepherd-fashion, over his left shoulder a patchwork jacket soaked with rain, while he was excitedly turning around in his brown hard fists a little felt hat, shrunken and discoloured by the wind and weather of many years. He had set down a long cudgel in front of the entrance.

When asked what he wanted, the man poured out, with wild grimaces, an incomprehensible flood of coarse sounds and words which indeed belonged to the dialect of that region, but to a special variety of it that seemed like a foreign tongue even to the housekeeper, though the latter had been born in Soana.

The young priest, who had attentively observed his visitor alongside the small lamp, endeavoured in vain to fathom the sense of his request. With much patience and by means of numerous questions, he was finally able to get this much out of him: that he was the father of seven children, some of whom he would like to enrol in the young priest's school. Francesco asked: "Where do you come from?" And when the answer came abruptly – "I am from Soana" – the priest was astonished and said instantly, "That is not possible – I know everybody in this place, but I don't know you and your family."

The herdsman, farmer, or whatever he was, then gave a passionate description of the situation of his dwelling. He accompanied this by many gestures, out of which however Francesco could make no sense. He only said, "If you are an inhabitant of Soana and your children have reached the age fixed by law, they would have had to be in my school long before this, in any case. And I must surely have seen you or your wife or your children in the church, at mass or confession."

Here the man opened his eyes wide and pressed his lips together. Instead of any answer he expelled his breath as from an outraged and burdened breast.

"Well, then, I will write down your name. I think it good of you to come yourself and take steps to see that your children may not remain ignorant and perhaps godless." At these words of the young priest the ragged visitor began to groan in a strange, almost animal fashion, so that his brown, sinewy and almost athletic body was shaken by it.

"Yes, indeed," repeated Francesco, taken aback. "I will write down your name and make enquiries into the matter." One could see tear after tear running from the reddened eyelids of the stranger over his unkempt face.

"Very well," said Francesco, who could not explain to himself the agitated conduct of his visitor – and, besides, was rather disturbed than touched by it, "very well, your case will be investigated. Just tell me your name, my good man, and send me your children tomorrow." At these words the man was silent and looked for a long time at Francesco with a helpless and tortured expression. The latter asked again, "What is your name? Tell me your name."

The priest had been struck from the very beginning by some element of fear, an air of being hunted, in the movements of his guest. Now that he was to give his name, and when at the same time the footsteps of Petronilla were heard outside on the stone floor, he ducked and revealed in other ways a terror such as is usually found only in lunatics or criminals. He seemed persecuted. He seemed to be fleeing from the police.

Nevertheless he seized a piece of paper and the priest's pen, stepped into the darkness, strangely enough, away from the light and over to the window. The sound from a nearby brook reached them, and from a greater distance came the roar of the waterfall of Soana. He traced with some difficulty, but legibly, something which he handed to the priest with an effort of the will. The latter said "All right", and, making the sign of the cross, "Go in peace." The uncouth fellow departed, leaving behind him a cloud of vapours which were redolent of salami, onions, wood smoke, he-goats and cow stables. As soon as he was gone, Francesco threw the window open.

The next morning Francesco said mass as usual, then rested a little, then ate his frugal breakfast, and soon thereafter was on his way to see the Sindaco,* whom one must visit early in order to find him at home – for he rode daily from a railroad station far below on the lake shore into Lugano, where he conducted on one of the busiest streets a wholesale and retail business in Ticino cheese.

The sun was shining on the little square, set with chestnut trees which were still bare. The square lay close by the church and constituted a sort of agora for the village. Upon some stone benches children were sitting and playing, while the mothers and older daughters were gathered about an antique marble sarcophagus overflowing with a copious supply of cold mountain water. They were washing clothes or carrying them away in baskets to dry. The ground was wet, for rain mingled with snowflakes had fallen the day before, and indeed it was under new-fallen snow that the tremendous rocky slope of Monte Generoso, with its inaccessible crags, towered up beyond the gorge in its own shadow and wafted fresh, snow-laden air across to Soana.

The young priest walked with downcast eyes past the washing women, whose loud greeting he answered with a nod. Looking over his glasses like an old man at the children who thronged about him, he gave them his hand for a moment. They all touched their lips to it eagerly and hastily. The part of the village which lay behind the square was made accessible by a number of narrow lanes. But even the main street could be used only by small vehicles, and only the first stretch of that. Towards the end of the village it narrowed, and moreover became so steep that one could get through and up it at best only with a laden mule. On this little street stood a small shop and the Swiss post office.

The postmaster, who had been on terms of the greatest comradeship with Francesco's predecessor, greeted him and was greeted in return, but yet in such a way as to keep the full distance between the seriousness of the consecrated priest and the trivial friendliness of the layman. Not far from the post office the priest turned into a pitiful little side alley, which descended in breakneck fashion by means of big and little flights of steps, past open goat stables and all sorts of dirty, windowless, cellar-like cavities. Chickens cackled, cats perched on rotten galleries amid bunches of suspended ears of corn. Here and there a goat bleated or a cow lowed, having for some reason or other not been taken out to pasture.

It was astonishing when you issued from these surroundings and, entering the house of the mayor through a narrow portal, found yourself in a flight of small vaulted chambers, the ceilings of which had been profusely painted by artisans with figures in the style of Tiepolo.* High windows and French doors, adorned with long red curtains, led from these sunny rooms out onto an equally sunny open terrace, which was set off by wonderful laurel and cone-shaped box trees of great age. Here, too, you heard the entrancing roar of the waterfall, as you did everywhere, and had the wild mountainside facing you across the valley.

The Sindaco, Sor Domenico, was a well-dressed, quiet man in his mid-forties, who had married for the second time scarcely three months before. His beautiful, blooming, twenty-two-year-old wife, whom Francesco had encountered in the kitchen, busy with the preparation of the breakfast, led him in to see her husband. When the latter had heard the priest tell of the visit which he had received the evening before, and had read the slip which bore in awkward characters the name of the uncouth visitor, a smile passed over his features. Then he made the young priest sit down and began in a perfectly matter-of-fact way, the mask-like indifference of his features quite undisturbed throughout his speech, to give the desired information about the mysterious visitor, who actually was a citizen of Soana who had hitherto remained unknown to the pastor.

"Luchino Scarabota," said the Sindaco – it was the name which the pastor's visitor had scribbled on the paper – "is by no means a poor man, but for years now his domestic affairs have been giving me and the entire parish the utmost concern, and there is really no telling where the whole thing will ultimately end. He belongs to an ancient family, and it is very probable that he has in him some of the blood of the famous Luchino Scarabota da Milano, who built during the fifteenth century the nave of the cathedral down in Como. We have a number of famous old names in our small district, Father, as you know."

While he spoke, the Sindaco had opened the French doors and led the pastor out onto the terrace, where he pointed out to him with a slightly raised hand in the steep, funnel-shaped spring of the waterfall one of those huts, hewn out of rough stone, such as the peasants of the district inhabited. But this hovel, lying at a great height, far above all the other houses, was distinguished from them not only by its isolated, seemingly inaccessible situation, but also by its smallness and shabbiness.

"Look where I am pointing my finger – that is where this Scarabota lives," said the Sindaco.

"I am surprised, Father," the speaker continued, "that you should not have heard anything as yet about that Alp and the people who live there. They have been causing the most hateful scandal all over the countryside for a decade and more. Unfortunately, we can get no hold on them. The woman has been brought into court and has claimed that the seven children she has borne – could anything be more absurd? – are not those of the man she lives with, but of summer tourists from Switzerland, who have to go past that Alp when they climb Monte Generoso. And mind you, the jade is covered with lice and dirt and is as repulsively ugly as sin.

"No, it is common knowledge that the man who visited you yesterday, and with whom she lives, is the father of her children. But that is the point: this man is at the same time her blood brother."

The young priest turned pale.

"Of course, this incestuous couple is avoided and outlawed by everybody. In this respect the *vox populi* rarely errs." With this explanation the Sindaco continued his account. "As often as one of the children has shown itself here, say in Arogno or Melano, it has been stoned nearly to death. Wherever these people are known, any church which the notorious couple enters is regarded as desecrated; and the two outlaws were made to feel it in so terrible a way, when they once thought they might make the attempt, that for years they have lost all inclination to go to church. And should it be permitted, do you think, that such children, such accursed creatures, who are a horror and a dread to everyone, should come down here to our school and sit on the same bench with the children of good Christians? Can it be fairly asked of us that we should permit our entire village, big and little, to be tainted by these products of moral infamy – these wicked, mangy beasts?"

The pale face of Father Francesco betrayed by no change of expression what impression the narrative of Sor Domenico had made on him. He thanked him and went away, showing in his whole bearing the same dignified seriousness with which he had come.

Soon after his conference with the Sindaco, Francesco made a report to his bishop on the Scarabota case. A week later the answer of the bishop was in his hand, ordering the young priest to get information in person with regard to the general state of things on the Alp of Santa Croce, as it was called. At the same time, the bishop praised the spiritual zeal of the young man and confirmed him in the feeling that he had every reason to feel his conscience oppressed on account of these erring and outlawed souls, and to be concerned for their salvation. From the blessings and consolations of Mother Church one must exclude no sinner, however far astray.

Not till about the end of March did official duties and also the condition of the snow on Monte Generoso permit the young priest of Soana, with a farmer as a guide, to undertake the ascent to the Alp of Santa Croce. Easter was close at hand, and although along the steep side of the gigantic mountain avalanches were constantly rolling with hollow thunder down into the gorge below the waterfall, yet wherever the sun had been able to work unchecked the spring had set in with full power.

Unlike his namesake of Assisi, Francesco was not a great lover of nature; still, all the tender, sap-laden things which were sprouting, leafing and blooming about him could not but affect him. Without the young man's needing to be clearly conscious of it, he had the fine stirrings of spring in his blood, and enjoyed his share of that inward swelling and urgency of all nature, which is of heavenly origin, and which, despite its rapturously sensuous earthly manifestations, is heavenly too in all the joys that blossom out of it.

On the square over which the priest first had to walk with his guide, the chestnut trees had stretched out delicate green little hands from brown, sticky buds. The children were noisy, and the sparrows no less so, nesting under the church roof and in countless nooks and crannies of the many-cornered village. The first swallows were executing their broad loops from Soana across the abyss of the gorge, where they seemed to swerve aside close to the fantastically turreted, inaccessible rocky masses of the mountain wall. High up on ledges and in holes of the rocks, where no human foot had ever gone, ospreys had their eyries. The great brown couples undertook glorious cruises and floated, merely for the sake of floating, for hours in endurance flights above the mountain peaks, circling ever higher and higher, as if they wished, in self-forgetting majesty, to soar out into the untrammelled infinity of space.

Everywhere, not only in the air, not only in the earth, upturned and brown or robed with grass and narcissus, not only in all that the earth sent upwards through stems and trunks into leaves and blossoms, but also in man there was a festal feeling, and the brown faces of the farmers working on the terraces between the rows of vines with hoe or curved knife shone with the light of Sunday: for most of them had already slaughtered the Easter-lamb, as they called it – that is, a young kid – and hung it up on the doorpost at home, with its legs tied together.

The women grouped about the overflowing marble sarcophagus, especially numerous and noisy today with their heaping wash-baskets, interrupted their clamorous merriment as the priest and his guide went by. There were also washerwomen standing at the exit from the village, where a stream of water gushed out of the rocks under a small image of the Virgin and flowed into a similar sarcophagus. Both this and the one that stood on the square had been taken out of the ground some time before in an orchard full of thousand-year-old holm oaks and chestnuts, where they had stood since time immemorial, barely emerging from the ground and hidden under ivy and wild laurel.

In passing, Francesco crossed himself – indeed, he interrupted his walk for a moment – to render homage with a genuflection to the Madonnetta above the sarcophagus, prettily surrounded with the wild flowers brought by the peasants. It was the first time he had seen this lovely little shrine, with the bees humming about it, for he had never yet visited this upper part of the village. The lower part of Soana, with its church and some pretty dwellings adorned with green shutters surrounding the chestnut-tree square, itself built up by masonry-supported terraces, was of almost middle-class prosperity, and in it big and little gardens displayed blossoming almond and orange trees and tall cypresses – in short, a more southern vegetation; but up here, a few hundred paces higher, it was nothing but an impoverished alpine village of herders, smelling of goats and cow stables. Then, too, there began here an extremely steep mountain road paved with slabs of trap-rock, tramped smooth by the outgoing and incoming of the great communal flock of goats at morning and evening – for it led up and out to the village common in the kettle-shaped district that fed the brook Savaglia, which forms farther down the glorious waterfall of Soana, and after a short roaring passage through a deep gorge sinks into the Lake of Lugano.

After the priest had climbed up a short time on this mountain road, always under the guidance of his companion, he stopped to take breath. Taking his big black plate-shaped hat from his head with his left hand, he drew with his right a large gay-coloured kerchief from his cassock, with which he dabbed the beads of sweat from his forehead. In general, the love of nature in an Italian priest – his feeling for the beauty of the landscape – is not great. But the distant view from a great height, a so-called bird's-eye view, does have a charm which seizes at times even the most unsophisticated and wrests from him a certain astonishment. Far below him Francesco spied his church with its surrounding village, at this height looking no bigger than a miniature, while round about him the titanic mountain world seemed to tower higher and higher into the heavens. With his springtime sensations was mingled now a consciousness of the sublime, which may perhaps originate in a comparison of our own pettiness with the oppressively monstrous works of nature and their mute threatening nearness, while this is combined with a partial realization of the fact that we too, after all, have some sort of share in this almightiness. In short, Francesco felt sublimely great and infinitely small at one and the same instant, and this led him to make on forehead and breast, with accustomed gesture, the sign of the cross that shields from errors and demons.

As he continued the ascent, religious problems and the practical ecclesiastical affairs of his parish soon took possession of the eager young cleric once more. And as he again stopped and turned around, this time at the entrance to a rocky mountain valley, the sight of a sadly neglected stonework shrine, erected here for the herders, gave him the idea of going to see all the existing shrines of his parish, however remote they might be, and putting them into a condition worthy of their sacred purpose. At once he began looking round him, searching for a vantage point that might command a view of all the existing shrines.

He took his own church with its attached parsonage as his starting point. As has been said before, it stood on the level of the village square, and its outer walls were continued downwards in the steep sides of its foundation rocks, along the bottom of which a merry mountain brook tumbled cheerfully. This brook, flowing through a channel underneath the Soana square, came out into the light through a stone arch, where it watered orchards and flowery meadows, though to be sure seriously fouled by waste water. Beyond the church and a little higher – though that was not ascertainable from this point – stood, on a round, level-terraced hill, the oldest sanctuary in the neighbourhood: a small chapel consecrated to the Virgin Mary, whose duty image on the altar was overarched by a Byzantine mosaic in the apse. This mosaic, its gold ground and design well preserved despite being more than a thousand years old, represented Christus Pantocrator. The distance from the main church to this shrine was not more than thrice a stone's throw. Another pretty chapel, consecrated to St Anna, stood at the same distance from it. Over and behind Soana rose a sharply pointed mountain peak, which of course was encircled by broad valley-lands and the flanks of the overtowering chain of Monte Generoso. This mountain, almost like a sugarloaf in shape, and seemingly inaccessible but green to the top, was called St Agata, because it housed on its peak a little chapel of that saint, to be used in emergencies. This made in the immediate vicinity of the village one church and three chapels. In addition, there were three or four other chapels in the outskirts. On every hill, at every pretty turn of the road, upon every peak with a view into the distance, here and there by picturesque rocky precipices, far and near over gorge and lake, pious centuries had affixed houses of God, so that in this respect the deep and universal piety of heathendom, which in the course of past millenniums had originally consecrated all these spots, was still to be felt, and thus created for itself divine allies against the threatening, terrible powers of that savage nature.

The young zealot looked with satisfaction upon all these institutions of Roman Catholic Christianity, such as distinguish the entire canton of Ticino. To be sure, he also had to admit, with the pain of the true champion of God, that they did not always command an active, living and pure faith, nor even enough love and concern, on the part of his associates, to preserve all these scattered heavenly dwelling places from neglect and forgetfulness.

After some time, they turned off into the narrow footpath which leads, after three hours of laborious ascent, to the summit of Generoso. In doing so, they very soon had to cross the bed of the Savaglia on a tumbledown bridge, in whose immediate proximity was the reservoir of the little brook, which plunged downwards a hundred yards and more in the fissure made by its own erosion. Here Francesco heard from various heights, depths and directions, together with the rushing of the mountain waters hastening down to their reservoir, the tinkle of the goat bells, and saw a man of coarse appearance – it was the communal herder of Soana – who, stretched at full length on the ground, supporting himself on the bank with his hands, his head bent down to the water's level, was quenching his thirst like an animal. Behind him were grazing some she-goats with their kids, while a wolfhound was waiting with pricked-up ears for orders and the moment when his lord and master should be done with drinking. "I too am a herder," thought Francesco. The man rose from the ground, whistled shrilly through his fingers, the sound re-echoing from the rock walls, and threw stones off into the distance, trying to frighten some of his widely scattered animals, to drive others onwards, or to recall still others, in order to save them from the danger of falling over the ledge. Francesco thought what a laborious and responsible task this was, even with animals – to say nothing of men, who were at all times exposed to the temptation of Satan.

The priest now resumed the ascent with redoubled zeal, as though there were danger that the Devil might perhaps be swifter than he on this road to his straying sheep. He had been trudging up for an hour or more, higher and higher into the rocky wilds of Generoso, guided all the while by his escort, with whom Francesco did not deign to converse. Suddenly he saw the Alp of Santa Croce lying fifty paces before him.

He could not believe that that heap of stones and the masonry in the midst of it, built up without mortar out of flat stone slabs, was the place which the guide had assured him he was seeking. What he had expected, after the words of the Sindaco, was a certain prosperity, whereas this dwelling could at most pass for a sort of shelter for sheep and goats in a sudden storm. Since it stood on a steep slope composed of rocky debris and jagged boulders, and since the zigzag course of the path to it was concealed, there appeared to be no access to the accursed spot. The young priest fought down his astonishment and a certain feeling of horror; he moved closer; and now, for the first time, the sight of this avoided and outlawed abode took on a somewhat more pleasing aspect.

Indeed, the decayed building was actually transformed before the eyes of the approaching priest into sheer loveliness, for it seemed as if the mass of boulders and debris let loose at a great height were dammed and contained by the rough-hewn square dwelling, so that beneath it there remained a stoneless slope of lush green, on which yellow cowslips of the most delicate beauty climbed in delightful profusion up to the platform in front of the house door – and, as if they were inquisitive, across the platform and literally through the house door into the outlawed cave itself.

At this sight Francesco started. This charge of yellow meadow flowers up against the ill-reputed threshold, this blooming ascent of luxuriant processions of long-stemmed forget-me-nots, under which veins of mountain water seeped away, and which likewise sought to take possession of the door with their blue reflection of the sky, seemed to him almost an open protest against human banishment, excommunication and law courts. In his astonishment, which was followed by a certain confusion, Francesco had to seat himself in his black cassock on a sun-warmed boulder. He had spent his youth in the lowlands, for the most part pent up in rooms, church, auditorium or study. His feeling for nature had not been aroused. He had never before carried out an expedition like this, into the stern, exalted loveliness of the high mountains; and he would perhaps never have done it if this combination of chance and duty had not urged the mountain journey upon him. Now he was overwhelmed by the novelty and grandeur of his impressions.

For the first time the young priest Francesco Vela felt a clear and transcendent sensation of existence surging through him, making him completely forget at times that he was a priest, and why he had come. All his notions of piety, which were intertwined with a quantity of Church rules and dogmas, had been not only displaced by this sensation, but extinguished. At this point he even forgot to cross himself. Below him lay the beautiful Lugano district of the upper Italian Alps, Sant'Agata with its pilgrim-haunted chapel, over which the brown ospreys were still circling, and the mountain of San Giorgio; there rose up the peak of Monte San Salvatore, and finally there lay below him, so far below as to make one giddy, carefully fitted into the valleys of the mountain relief like an elongated sheet of glass, the arm of the Lake of Lugano known as Capolago – on it the sailing boat of a fisher which looked like a tiny moth on a hand mirror. Behind all this, the white peaks of the High Alps had, as it were, climbed higher and higher with Francesco. From among them rose the white Monte Rosa, with seven white peaks before it, glistening against the silky blue of the azure like a diadem and a mirage.

If one may justly speak of a mountain sickness, so one may speak with no less justification of a condition which befalls men on mountain heights, and which one may best designate as incomparable health. This health the young priest now experienced in his own blood, like a rejuvenation. Beside him, between stones and among the still barren heather, stood a little flower the like of which Francesco had never seen in his life. It was an extremely lovely species of blue gentian, whose petals were painted with a surprisingly delicious flaming blue. The young man in the black cassock left the little flower, which he had started to pluck in the first joy of his discovery, standing unmolested in its modest place, and merely pushed the heather plants aside, in order to study the miracle for a long time and with rapture. Everywhere there pushed up between the stones young, light-green leaves of the dwarf beech, and from a certain distance, across the slopes of hard grey rubble and tender green, the flocks of the wretched Luchino Scarabota announced themselves by their tinkling bells. This entire mountain world had a primitive strangeness, the youthful charm of bygone human ages, of which there was no longer any trace left in the low valleys.

Francesco had sent his guide home, as he wished to make the return trip undisturbed by the presence of anyone, and moreover did not want any witness of what he was planning to do at the hearth of Luchino. In the meantime, he had already been observed, and a number of dirty children's heads, with matted hair, were thrust out again and again in curiosity from the smoke-blackened hole that served as door to Scarabota's stone citadel.

Slowly the priest began to approach it, and entered the perimeter of the building. Here he could see the great extent of the owner's livestock; the ground was littered by the droppings of a great herd of cattle and goats. Into Francesco's nose penetrated more and more strongly, together with the powerful, rarefied mountain air, the smell of those animals, whose increasing pungency was rendered tolerable at the entrance to the dwelling by the charcoal smoke that forced its way out at the same time. When he appeared in the frame of the door, cutting off the light with his black cassock, the children retreated into the darkness, where they met with silence the greeting and all the other salutations of the priest, who did not see them. Only an old she-goat came up, bleated softly and sniffed at him.

Gradually to the eye of God's messenger it had become lighter in the interior of the space. He saw a stable, filled with a high pile of manure and deepening at the rear into a natural cavern, which had been originally present in the gompholite, or whatever rock it was. In a rough stone partition on the right a passage had been opened, through which the priest cast a glance at the now-forsaken family hearth: a mountain of ashes, the centre still full of coals, and heaped up on the rock floor, which lay exposed in its natural state. On a chain thickly coated with soot an equally sooty bossed copper kettle hung above the hearth. By this primitive fireplace stood a backless bench, whose broad seat, as thick as your fist, rested on two equally broad posts fastened in the rock, which for a century and more had been smoothed and polished by generations of tired herdsmen and their wives and children. The wood no longer seemed to be wood, but rather a polished yellow marble or soapstone, though with countless scars and cuts. The four-square room – which by the way, with its naturally untrimmed walls, built up of rough boulders and slabs of slate, looked more like a cave, and from which the smoke passed through the door into the stable and from there into the open, because it had no other outlet, unless perhaps through some leaks in the walls – was blackened by the smoke and soot of decades, so that one might almost fancy oneself in the interior of a chimney thickly coated with soot.

Francesco was just noting the peculiar gleam of eyes that were shining out of a corner when a rolling and sliding of rubble became audible outside, and immediately afterwards the figure of Luchino Scarabota stepped like a noiseless shadow into the doorway. It shut out the sun, so that the room was still more pitch-dark. The uncouth mountain herder was breathing heavily, not only because he had traversed in a short time the distance from a remote, more elevated Alp after he had spotted from there the priest's arrival, but because this visit was an event for the outlawed man.

The greeting was short. Francesco was asked to sit down by his host, after the latter had with his rough hands cleared the soapstone bench of the stones and cowslips which served his accursed brood as playthings.

The mountain herder stirred the fire and blew upon it with puffed cheeks, whereat his feverish eyes gleamed still more wildly in the reflected light. He nursed the flame with logs and dry brushwood, so that the pungent smoke was enough to drive out the priest. The herdsman was obsequious and submissive; he acted with a nervous eagerness, much as if everything now depended on not losing by some wrong move the favour of the higher being that had entered his poor dwelling. He brought out a great pail full of milk, which was covered with a thick layer of cream, but was unfortunately so badly fouled that for that reason alone Francesco was unable to touch it. Although he was hungry, he also declined to partake of fresh cheese and clean bread, because he had a superstitious fear of committing a sin by eating it. Finally, when the mountaineer had somewhat composed himself and was standing facing him with fearful expectant eyes and limp arms, the priest began to speak as follows:

"Luchino Scarabota, you are not to be deprived of the consolation of our Holy Church, and your children shall hereafter not be cast out of the community of Catholic Christians, if it turns out, first of all, that the evil rumours touching you are untrue, and if you honestly confess, show penitence and contrition, and are prepared with God's aid to remove the stumbling block. Therefore, first open your heart to me, Scarabota: confess freely in what respect you are calumniated, and confess with honest truth the thing that is burdening you."

After this speech the herdsman was silent. Only a brief wild sound was suddenly wrung from his throat. It betrayed no feeling, however, but had rather a gurgling, bird-like quality. With the fluency of familiarity, Francesco at once proceeded to hold up before the sinner the terrible consequences of obduracy and the propitiatory goodness and love of God the Father, which he had proved through the sacrifice of his only Son, the sacrifice of the Lamb which took the sins of the world upon itself. Through Jesus Christ, he concluded, any sin can be forgiven, provided that an unreserved confession, combined with remorse and prayer, has proven to our Heavenly Father the contrition of the miserable sinner.

The priest had waited a long time and was rising with a shrug of the shoulders, as though he intended to leave; then finally the herder began to mumble out an incomprehensible tangle of words: a sort of gurgling like that of a disgorging hawk. And with straining attention the priest attempted to make out as much as possible from his muddled speech. But what he could understand seemed to him quite as strange and remarkable as what was obscure. Only this much became clear from all the alarming and oppressive imaginary things he said – that Luchino Scarabota wished to secure his aid against all kinds of devils that lived in the mountains and harassed him.

It would ill have become the credulous young priest to doubt the existence and activity of evil spirits. Was not creation filled with all manner and degree of fallen angels from the retinue of Lucifer, the rebel whom God had cast out? Yet here he felt horrified, not knowing whether it was at the mental darkness he was encountering, caused by unheard-of superstition, or whether it was at the hopeless blindness caused by ignorance. He resolved to ask some questions, in order to form a judgement as to his parishioner's range of ideas and the power of his understanding.

Then it soon became evident that this wild, neglected man knew nothing of God, still less of Jesus Christ the Saviour and least of all about the existence of a Holy Ghost. On the other hand, it seemed as if he felt himself surrounded by demons and was possessed by a gloomy feeling of persecution. And in the priest he did not see the chosen servant of God at all, but rather a mighty sorcerer or God himself. What could Francesco do but cross himself, while the herder humbly threw himself on the ground and with moist, protruding lips began to lick his shoes like an idolater, and to cover them with kisses?

The young priest had never found himself in such a situation. The rarefied mountain air, the spring, the separation from the usual level of civilization, all this had the effect of clouding his consciousness. Something like a visionary spell entered the sphere of his soul, where reality was dissolving into unstable, airy forms. This alteration was combined with a faint fearfulness, which suggested to him more than once a precipitate flight down into the realm of consecrated churches and chimes. The Devil was powerful: who could know how many ways and means he had of luring onwards the most unsuspecting, most faithful Christian, and hurling him down from the brink of a giddy height into the abyss?

Francesco had not been taught that the idols of the heathen were nothing but empty creations of the imagination. The Church expressly recognized their power – but it represented it as one hostile to God. They were still fighting with Almighty God, though hopelessly, for the world. Hence the pale young priest was not a little startled when his host fetched a wooden article out of some nook in his dwelling, a horrible carving which was no doubt a fetish. Despite his priestly horror of the lascivious object,

Francesco could not refrain from taking a closer look at it. With abhorrence and astonishment, he confessed to himself that the most revolting heathenish abomination, namely the rural worship of Priapus,* was still active here. Nothing but Priapus, it was clearly evident, could be represented by this primitive religious emblem.

Scarcely had Francesco seized the harmless little god of procreation, the god of rural fertility, who was so openly accorded high honour by the ancients, when the strange constriction of his soul turned into holy wrath. Without stopping to think, he flung the obscene little piece of mandrake into the fire, from which the herder, rushing forwards as swiftly as a dog, drew it out again in the same instant. It was glowing in spots, and in other spots it was flaming, but the rough hands of the pagan immediately restored it to safety. But now, along with its deliverer, it had to undergo a torrent of castigating words.

Luchino Scarabota did not seem to know which of the two gods he should regard as the stronger: the wooden one or the one of flesh and blood. However, he kept his eyes, in which horror and terror were mingled with spiteful rage, fixed on the new deity, whose atrocious daring did not, at any rate, point to any sense of weakness. Once started, the emissary of the one and only God did not allow himself to be intimidated in his sacred zeal by the glances, threatening as they were, of the benighted idolater. And without any ceremony he now came to speak of the heinous sin from which, as everyone said, the numerous progeny of the mountaineer had sprung.

Amid the young priest's loud words burst in, as it were, the sister of Scarabota – but without saying anything, and merely eyeing the zealot in secret, she busied herself here and there in the cave-like dwelling. She was a pale and repulsive woman, to whom washing seemed to be a thing unknown. One had disagreeable glimpses of her naked body through the rents of her neglected clothing.

After the priest had finished and had temporarily exhausted his store of stinging reproaches, the woman sent her brother out into the open with a short, barely audible word. Without objection, the savage disappeared like the most obedient hound. Then the filth-encrusted sinner, whose matted black hair hung down over her broad hips, kissed the priest's hand with the words, "Praised be Jesus Christ!"

Then she instantly burst into tears.

She said the priest was quite right to condemn her with harsh words. She had indeed sinned against the word of God – though not at all in the way indicated by the calumnies told about her. She alone was the sinner: her brother, instead, was wholly innocent. She swore, and by all the saints, that she had never been guilty of that frightful sin of which she was accused – incest. To be sure, she had lived unchastely, and as she was now confessing, she was ready to describe the fathers of her children, if not to call them all by name. For she knew very few of the names, since need had often caused her to sell her favours, she said, to passing strangers.

For the rest, she had brought her children into the world painfully and without any help, and some she had had to bury shortly after their birth, here and there in the rubble of Monte Generoso. Whether he could give her absolution or not, she knew nevertheless that God had forgiven her, for she had done penance enough through privations, sufferings and cares.

Francesco could not but regard the tearful confession of the woman as a tissue of lies – at least so far as the incest was concerned. To be sure, he felt that there were actions which it is absolutely repugnant to confess before men, and which God alone learns in the solitary stillness of prayer. He respected this reserve in the degenerate woman, and could not conceal from himself that in many respects she was of a higher type than her brother. In the manner of her justification there was a great resoluteness. Her eye confessed, but neither kind urgency nor the glowing pincers of the executioner would have wrested from her a confession in words. It was she, as it turned out, that had sent the man to Francesco. She had seen the pale young priest when she went to market one day at Lugano, where she sold the products of her mountain farm, and at sight of him she had taken courage, and had conceived the idea of recommending her outlawed children to his mercy. She alone was the head of the family and cared for her brother and her children.

"I will not discuss," said Francesco, "how far you are guilty or innocent. One thing is certain: if you do not wish your children to grow up like beasts, you must separate from your brother. As long as you live with him, the frightful reputation you have can never be lived down. People will always assume that you have committed that terrible sin."

After these words, obstinacy and defiance seemed to take hold of the woman – at any rate, she made no answer for a long time, as if no stranger were present, devoting herself to her household duties. Meanwhile, a girl of about fifteen came in, drove some goats into the opening of the stable and then began to help the woman, also as if Francesco were not there. The young priest knew at once, as soon as he merely saw the girl's shadow gliding through the depths of the cave, that she must be of uncommon beauty. He crossed himself, for he felt in his body a faint dread of an inexplicable kind. He did not know whether he should resume his admonitions in the presence of the youthful shepherdess. To be sure, there could be no doubt that she was depraved to the core, since Satan had called her to life by the way of the blackest sin, but still there might be a remnant of purity left in her, and who could know whether she had any idea of her murky origin?

Her movements, at any rate, displayed great calmness, from which one could certainly not conclude that she had an uneasy mind or a burden on her conscience. On the contrary, everything about her was of a modest self-assurance, which was not affected by the presence of the pastor. She had so far not cast a glance at Francesco – at least, not so that he had met her eye or otherwise caught her looking at him. Indeed, while he himself was secretly watching her through his glasses, he had to cast more and more doubt on the idea that a child of sin, a child of such parents, could really be so formed. At last she vanished up a ladder into a sort of attic, so that Francesco could now continue his laborious pastoral work.

"I cannot leave my brother," said the woman, "and for the very simple reason that he is helpless without me. He can sort of write his name, and I taught him that only with the greatest difficulty. He does not know coins, and he is afraid of the railway, the city and people. If I go away, he will pursue me as a wretched dog pursues his lost master. He will either find me or perish miserably – and then what is to become of the children and our property? If I stay here with the children, then I'd like to see the man who could succeed in getting my brother away – unless they should put him in chains and lock him up in Milan behind iron bars."

The priest said, "That may yet come to pass if you will not take my good advice."

Then the woman's fears turned into rage. She had sent her brother to Francesco so that he might take pity on them, not to make them unhappy. In that case, she would certainly rather go on living as they had until now: hated and cast out by the people down below. She was a good Catholic, but if the Church cast out a man, he had a right to sell himself to the Devil. And what she had not yet done – the great sin with which she was charged – she might then actually commit.

Together with the muffled words of the woman, interspersed with sudden outcries, Francesco kept hearing from above, where the girl had disappeared, a sweet singing – now like the softest breath, now increasing in intensity – so that his soul was more under the spell of this melody than intent upon the furious outbursts of the woman. And a hot wave rose up in him, combined with an anxiety such as he had never felt before. The smoky hole of this animal-human dwelling-stable seemed to be transformed, as by enchantment, into the loveliest of all the crystalline grottoes of Dante's Paradise – full of angel voices and the flutter of pinions, which sounded like those of the laughing dove.

He went out. It was impossible for him to withstand any longer, without trembling visibly, such confusing influences. Outside, emerging in front of the excavated-stone pile, he inhaled the freshness of the mountain air and was immediately filled, like an empty vessel, with the mighty impression of the mountain world. His soul became transferred, as it were, into the farthest ranges of his eyesight, and consisted of the colossal masses of the earth's crust, from distant, snowy peaks to nearby, terrible abysses, under the royal brightness of the spring day. Still he saw the brown ospreys describing their unconscious circles above the sugarloaf of Sant'Agata. Then he hit upon the idea of holding a secret service for the outlawed family up there, and laid this plan before the woman, who had stepped dejectedly upon the threshold of the cave, about which dandelions were clustering. "To Soana you cannot venture, as you well know," said he, "and if I should invite you there, it would be a great mistake for both of us."

Again the woman was moved to tears, and promised to appear before the chapel of Sant'Agata on a certain day with her brother and the older children.

When the young priest had gone far enough away from the vicinity of the dwelling place of Luchino Scarabota and his curse-laden family so that he could not longer be seen from there, he chose a sun-warmed boulder to rest on, while he thought over what he had just experienced. He told himself that he had ascended there with a thrill of interest, to be sure, but yet with a dutifully sober mind and without any foretaste of that which was now disquieting him in such an ominous manner. What was it? He smoothed, brushed and picked at his cassock for a long time, as if this would enable him to extract the secret.

When some time had elapsed and he had still not yet felt the desired enlightenment, he took his breviary from his pocket, as was his wont, but even though he at once began to read aloud, it did not free him from a certain strange irresoluteness. He felt as if he had forgotten to do something, some important part of his mission. Hence, from behind his glasses, he turned his eyes again and again towards the road with a certain expectancy, and could not summon up courage to continue the descent he had begun.

So he fell into a strange reverie, from which he was wakened by two small incidents which, to his overwrought imagination, took on an exaggerated significance. First, his right-hand lens cracked under the influence of the cold mountain air, and almost immediately afterwards he heard a fearful sneeze above his head and felt a heavy pressure on his shoulders.

The young priest sprang up. He laughed loudly when he recognized, as the cause of his panic, a spotted he-goat, which had given him a proof of its unlimited confidence by resting its fore hooves on his shoulders without any regard for his clerical garb.

But this was only the beginning of its most obtrusive familiarity. The shaggy buck with his strong, finely curved horns and his flashing eyes was accustomed, it seemed, to beg of passing mountain-climbers, and did this in such a droll, resolute and irresistible fashion that one could only get rid of him by running away. Again and again, rearing in the air, he set his hooves on Francesco's breast, and seemed determined, after the harassed priest had been forced to let him sniff his pockets and consume some breadcrumbs with ravenous greed, to nibble at the priest's hair, nose and fingers.

An old bearded she-goat, with bell and udder touching the ground, had followed the robber, and, encouraged by him, began to harass the priest likewise. Upon her the breviary with its gilt edges and cross had made a particular impression, and she succeeded, while Francesco was occupied with repelling a curving buck's horn, in getting possession of the little book – and, taking its black-printed leaves for green ones, she followed the prescription of the prophet and feasted literally and greedily upon the sacred verities.*

The annoyance was increased by the arrival of other animals which had been scattered about, grazing – then, of a sudden, the shepherdess appeared as his rescuer. It was the very same girl that Francesco had first casually seen in Luchino's hut. After she had driven off the goats, the strong, slender girl stood before him with freshly reddened cheeks and laughing eyes. He said, "You have saved me, my good child." And he added with a laugh of his own, as he received his breviary from the hands of young Eve, "It is really weird that, despite my pastoral office, I am so helpless against your flock."

A priest may not converse with a young girl or woman longer than his ecclesiastical duty may demand, and the parish remarks on it at once if he is seen in such a tête-à-tête outside the church. So, mindful of his stern calling, Francesco continued his journey homeward, without tarrying long – and yet he had the feeling that he had detected himself in a sin, and must purify himself at the next opportunity by a remorseful penance. He had not yet got beyond the reach of the herd-bells when the sound of a woman's voice came to his ears, suddenly making him forget once more all his meditations. The voice was of such a nature that he did not surmise that it might belong to the shepherdess he had just left behind. Francesco had not only heard in Rome the church choir in the Vatican, but had also often heard secular singers in Milan with his mother, years before, and so the coloratura and the *bel canto* of prima donnas were not unknown to him. Involuntarily, he stood still and waited. It must be tourists from Milan, he thought, and hoped perhaps in passing to get a glimpse of the possessor of this glorious voice. As she did not seem to come, he again carefully descended, step by step, down from the giddy heights into the valley below.

What Francesco had experienced on this official errand, as a whole and in particular, was not worth talking about if one does not take into consideration the abominations that had their breeding place in the hut of the miserable Scarabotas. But the young priest felt at once that this mountain trip had become an event of great significance in his life, even though he was for the moment far from realizing its entire import. He could trace a transformation that, working from within him, had taken place in his being. He found himself in a new state, which seemed stranger to him every minute, and somewhat suspicious, but yet nowhere near so suspicious as to scent Satan behind it, or perhaps to throw an inkpot at him, even if he had had one in his pocket. The mountain world lay below him like a paradise. For the very first time, with involuntarily folded hands, he congratulated himself on having been entrusted by his superiors with ministering just this parish. Compared with this delicious height and depth, what was Peter's vessel, which came down from Heaven with three angels holding the corners?* Where was there a greater majesty, from man's point of view, than these inaccessible crags of Monte Generoso, on which ever and again the dull springtime thunder of melting snow was audible in an avalanche?

From the day of his visit to the outlaws, Francesco, to his own astonishment, could no longer find the way back to the thoughtless peace of his former existence. The new aspect which nature had assumed for him did not fade away: again, and she would not permit herself to be driven back in any way into her former inanimate state. The manner of her influences, by which the priest was oppressed not only by day, but also in his dreams, he called and recognized at first as temptations. And as the faith of the Church had been fused with pagan superstition, just by the fact of having struggled against it, Francesco seriously attributed his transformation to the touching of that wooden object, that little piece of mandrake which the shaggy herdsman had rescued from the fire. Undoubtedly, there had still remained active a remnant of those abominations which the ancients reverenced under the name of phallic worship – that shameful cult which had been laid low in the world by the holy war of the cross of Jesus. Up to the time when he had set eyes on that disgusting object, the cross alone had been seared in Francesco's soul.

They had branded him, just exactly as they brand the sheep of a flock with a red-hot die, with the mark of the cross, and this mark had become, present alike in waking and in dreaming, the symbol of his own essence. Now the accursed and embodied Devil was looking down over the crosspiece of the cross, and that most unclean, horrible satyr-symbol was usurping more and more, in constant conflict, the place of the cross.

Francesco had reported to his bishop, as well as to the mayor, on the success of his pastoral visit, and the answer which he received from him was an approval of his procedure. "Above all," wrote the bishop, "let us avoid any open scandal." He found it extremely shrewd that Francesco had appointed a special and secret service for the poor sinners on Sant'Agata, in the chapel of Our Holy Mother Mary. But the approval of his superior could not restore the peace of Francesco's soul – he could not get rid of the idea that he had come back from up there with a kind of spell fastened upon him.

In Ligornetto, where Francesco was born, and where his uncle, the famous sculptor, had spent the last ten years of his life, there still lived the same old pastor who had initiated him as a boy into the saving truths of the Catholic faith, and had pointed out to him the paths of grace. This old priest he sought out one day, after he had walked the road from Soana to Ligornetto in about three hours. The old priest bade him welcome and was visibly touched as he agreed to hear the confession which the young man wished to make to him. Of course he absolved him.

Francesco's pangs of conscience are substantially expressed in the revelation which he made to the old man. He said,

"Since I was in the home of the wretched sinners on the Alp of Soana, I find myself under a kind of obsession. I shudder. I feel as if I had not only put on another coat, but actually another skin. When I hear the waterfall of Soana roaring, then I should like best to climb down into the deep gorge and place myself under the falling mass of water, for hours at a time, so as to become pure and healthy, as it were, inside and out. When I see the cross in the church, the cross over my bed, I laugh. I cannot weep as I used to when picturing to myself the sufferings of the Saviour. On the other hand, my eyes are attracted by all sorts of objects which are like Luchino Scarabota's one, made of mandrake. Sometimes they are quite unlike it, too, and I see a resemblance just the same. In order to study, in order to bury myself deeply in the study of the Church Fathers, I had curtains put up before the windows of my little room. Now I have taken them away. The singing of the birds, the roaring of the many brooks through the meadows past my house after the melting of the snow – yes, even the scent of the narcissus – used to disturb me. Now I open my double windows wide, in order to enjoy all this with veritable greediness.

"All this alarms me," Francesco had continued, "but there is worse yet. As if by black magic I have become a prey to unclean devils. Their tickling and prickling, their impudent prodding and provocation to sin, at every hour of the day and night, is terrible. I open the window, and through their sorcery it seems to me as if the songs of the birds in the blossoming cherry tree under my window were teeming with unchastity. Certain shapes in the bark of trees, and even certain lines of the mountains, remind me of parts of the *corpus femininum*.* It is a terrible assault of crafty, spiteful and odious demons, to which I am delivered up in spite of all my prayers and castigations. All nature – I tell you with horror – sometimes roars, bellows and thunders in my frightened ears one monstrous phallic song, through which, as I am forced to believe despite all my reluctance, it worships the miserable little wooden idol of the herder.

"All this, of course, increases my unrest and the torment of my soul." Francesco had proceeded, "the more so as I recognize it as my duty to march to battle as fighter against that pestilential herd up there on the Alp. But that is still not the worst part of my confession. Worse still, even in the duties most inseparable from my calling there is mingled, with an almost devilish sweetness, something like an all-perplexing, inextinguishable poison. Once I was moved with pure and holy zeal by the words of Jesus where he tells of the lost sheep and the shepherd who forsakes his flock in order to bring it back from the inaccessible cliffs.* But now I doubt whether this zeal of mine is as pure as I once thought it. I awake at night, my face bathed in tears, and everything within me is dissolved into sobbing compassion for the lost souls up yonder. But when I say 'lost souls', this is perhaps the point where a sharp line must be drawn between the false and the true – for the sinful souls of Scarabota and his sister are represented in my mind's eye simply and solely by the fruit of their sin – that is, their daughter.

"Now I ask myself whether unlawful desire for her is not the cause of my eagerness, and whether I am doing right and not running the risk of eternal death if I continue my apparently pious work."

Serious, but smiling at times, the old experienced priest had listened to the pedantic confession of the youth. This was the Francesco he knew, with his conscientious love of outward and inward order, and his craving for scrupulous accuracy and neatness. He said, "Francesco, be not afraid. Keep to the path you have always trodden. It must not surprise you if the machinations of the Evil Enemy appear to be most powerful and dangerous just at the time when you are proceeding to rob him of the victims that he already thought were safe, so to speak."

In a mood of relief Francesco stepped out of the parsonage into the street of the village of Ligornetto, in which he had spent his early youth. It is a little place, situated on a rather flat and broad valley floor and surrounded by fruitful fields, upon which, over the heads of vegetables and grain stalks, the grape vines are entwined back and forth from mulberry to mulberry like firmly twisted dark ropes. This locality is also dominated by the mighty crags of Monte Generoso, the west side of which here rises majestically from its base.

It was about midday, and Ligornetto was drowsy. Francesco was barely greeted on his way by a few cackling chickens, some playing children, and at the end of the village by a yelping dog. Here – that is, at the end of the village – the residence of his uncle closed the street like a door. It had been erected by a man of considerable means and was once the *buen retiro** of Vincenzo the sculptor. It was now uninhabited and had come into the possession of the canton of Ticino as a sort of memorial endowment. Francesco walked up the steps of the forsaken garden, where he yielded to a sudden desire to visit once again the interior of the house. Neighbouring farmers, old acquaintances, handed the key over to him.

The connections which the young priest had with the fine arts were the traditional ones of his rank. His famous uncle had been dead for about ten years, and since the day of his burial Francesco had not been inside the celebrated artist's home. He could not have said what suddenly moved him to visit the empty house, which he had hitherto mostly regarded only in passing and with fleeting interest. His uncle had never been more to him than a dignitary whose sphere of activity was an alien, meaningless thing.

When Francesco turned the key in the lock and stepped into the vestibule through the door that creaked on its rusty hinges, a faint shudder passed through him at the dust-laden stillness which was wafted towards him down the stairs and from all sides out of the open doors. Just to the right of the hall was the late artist's library, which revealed at once that an eager student had lived here. In low bookcases there were shelved here not only Vasari, but the complete works of Winckelmann, while the Italian Parnassus was represented by the sonnets of Michelangelo, and by Dante, Petrarch, Tasso, Ariosto and others.* In specially constructed cabinets a collection of drawings and etchings was housed, also one of Renaissance medallions and all sorts of valuable curios, among them painted Etruscan vases, and some other examples of ancient art in bronze and marble were set up in the room. Here and there on the wall hung in a frame a particularly fine drawing by Michelangelo or Leonardo, representing perhaps a male or female nude. One small cabinet had three of its sides filled almost from top to bottom with such objects.

From here one entered a domed rotunda, whose elevation traversed several storeys, and which got its light from above. Here Vincenzo had worked with modelling wood and chisel, and the plaster casts of his best works filled this almost churchly room – a crowded and mute assemblage.

Oppressed, even alarmed, and starting at the echo of his own footsteps, with a bad conscience, as it were, Francesco had got this far and now proceeded, really for the first time, to study this or that work of his uncle's. There was Ghiberti* to be seen beside a statue of Michelangelo. A Dante was there too. These works were covered with patterns of dots, as the models had been executed on a larger scale in marble. But these world-famed figures could not hold the attention of the young priest for long. Near them were the statues of three young girls, the daughters of a marquis, who had been sufficiently open-minded to let the master portray them in the nude. From all appearances, the youngest of the young ladies was not over twelve, the second not over fifteen, the third not over seventeen years old. Francesco only came to himself after he had surveyed the slender bodies for a long time in utter self-forgetfulness. These works did not display their nudity, like those of the Greeks, as a natural nobility and image of the deity, but one felt it as an indiscretion of the bedroom. In the first place, the copy of the originals had not been disassociated from them as persons, and had remained fully recognizable as such, and these originals seemed to say: "We have been indecently exposed and disrobed by brutal decree, contrary to our will and our sense of shame." When Francesco awoke from his absorption, his heart was pounding, and he looked fearfully in all directions. He was doing nothing wrong, but he felt it was a sin even to be alone with such creations.

He resolved to leave as quickly as possible, lest he should be actually caught there. Yet, when he had again reached the house door, he dropped the latch into the lock from the inside, instead of going away, and turned the key, so that he was now locked into the ghostly house of the dead man and could no longer be surprised by anybody. This done, he resumed his station before that scandal in plaster, the three graces.

His heart began to beat more violently, and a pale and fearful madness came over him. He felt impelled to stroke the hair of the oldest marchioness, as if she were living. Although this action plainly, and in his own judgement, bordered on insanity, yet it was still a priestly one, to a certain extent. But the second marchioness had to suffer more: a stroking of shoulder and arm – a round shoulder and a round arm, which ended in a soft and delicate hand. Soon Francesco, by more extended caressing of the third and youngest marchioness, and finally by a shy, sinful kiss under her left breast, had become a disconcerted, perplexed and penitent sinner, who was in no better frame of mind than Adam when he heard the voice of the Lord after he had eaten of the apple of knowledge. He fled. He ran away as if haunted.

The following days Francesco spent partly in the church praying, partly in his parsonage chastising himself. His penitence and his remorse were deep. By a fervour of worship such as he had not known hitherto he might hope to be victor in the end over the temptations of the flesh. Yet the struggle between the good and evil principle had burst out in his breast with undreamt-of frightfulness, so that it seemed to him that God and the Devil had for the first time transferred their battleground to his breast. Even the uncontrollable part of his existence, sleep, no longer offered the young cleric any peace, for that unguarded season of human repose seemed especially favourable to Satan for setting up seductive and pernicious delusions in the innocent soul of the young man. One night towards morning, he knew not whether it happened while sleeping or waking, he saw in the white light of the moon the three white figures of the lovely daughters of the marquis enter his room and approach his bed, and on looking closer he perceived that each one coalesced in a magical way with the image of the young shepherdess on the Alp of Santa Croce.

There was no doubt that from the little miniature dwelling of Scarabota down to the room of the priest, into which the Alp could look through the window, a connection had been established whose hemp was not spun by angels. Francesco knew enough of the heavenly hierarchy, as of the hellish one, to recognize at once whence this work had its source. Experienced in many a branch of scholastic science, he assumed that evil demons, in order to exert certain pernicious effects, make use of the influence of the stars. He had learnt that with respect to his body man belonged among the celestial spheres, that his reason made him the equal of the angels, that his will was subordinated to God, but that God permitted fallen angels to direct his will away from God, and that the realm of the demons was increased by alliance with such already perverted beings. Moreover, a temporary physical emotion, when exploited by the hellish spirits, could often be the cause of a man's eternal damnation. In short, the young priest quivered to the marrow of his bones in fear of the poisonous sting of the *diaboli*, the demons that reek of blood, of the bestial Behemoth,* and most especially of Asmodeus, the well-known demon of whoring.*

He could not at first imagine in the accursed incestuous couple the sin of witchcraft and sorcery. To be sure, he had one experience which seemed to him gravely suspicious. Every day he undertook with holy zeal and all the resources of religion a purification of his soul, in order to cleanse it of the image of the shepherd girl, and again and again she stood there more clearly, firmly and plainly than before. What sort of painting was it, and what sort of indestructible panel of wood was underneath it – or what sort of canvas was it on which one could not make the slightest impression either by water or fire?

The continual intrusion of this image became the object of his quiet and astounded observation. He would read a book, and when he saw on a page the soft countenance, framed in its peculiarly reddish earth-brown hair and gazing with wide dark eyes, he would cover it with a leaf previously inserted. But it passed through every leaf as if none were there, just as it made its way through curtains, doors and walls both in the house and in the church.

Amid such anxieties and inner struggle the young priest almost died of impatience, for the appointed date of the special service on the peak of Sant'Agata would not come quickly enough. He wished to do the duty he had undertaken as quickly as possible, because he might perhaps in that way wrest the girl from the talons of the prince of hell. He wished still more to see the girl again, but what he desired most was his liberation, which he confidently expected, from the torment of being under a spell. Francesco ate little, spent the greater part of his nights in wakefulness and, becoming daily more haggard and pale, was more than ever invested by his parish with the odour of an exemplary piety.

The morning had come at last on which the pastor had his appointment with the poor sinners in the chapel that stood high up on the sugarloaf of Sant'Agata. The extremely arduous path to the chapel could not be traversed in less than two hours. At the ninth hour Francesco stepped out into the square of Soana, ready for the trip, with his heart cheered and refreshed, and surveying the world with newborn eyes. It was nearing the first of May. Nothing more delicious could be imagined than this day which was just beginning, but the young man had often lived through days of equal beauty before this without feeling, as he did today, as if Nature were the very garden of Eden. Today he was in the midst of Paradise.

Women and girls were standing as usual about the sarcophagus, with its flow of clear mountain water, and saluted the priest with loud cries. Something in his bearing and his mien, as well as the holy-day freshness of the young day, had given the laundresses courage. With skirts wedged between their legs, so that in some cases the brown calves and knees were visible, they stood bending over, working stoutly with their equally brown, powerful bare arms. Francesco stepped up to the group. He felt induced to say all kinds of friendly things that in no case bore any relation to his pastoral office, about good weather, good spirits and the hope of a good wine crop. For the first time, probably stimulated by his visit to the house of his uncle the sculptor, the young priest deigned to inspect the ornamental frieze on the sarcophagus, which consisted of a bacchanalian procession and showed prancing satyrs, dancing female flutists and the tiger-drawn chariot of Dionysus, the grape-crowned god of wine. At this moment it did not seem strange to him that the ancients had covered the stone shroud of death with the figures of ebullient life. The women and girls, among whom there were some of unusual beauty, chattered and laughed into the sarcophagus during this inspection, and at times it seemed to him that he himself was surrounded by shouting, intoxicated maenads.

This second ascent into the mountain-world compared with the first one, was like that of a man with open eyes compared to that of one who had been blind from the womb. Francesco felt with compelling clearness that he had suddenly had his eyes opened. In this respect the inspection of the sarcophagus seemed to him not an accident at all, but deeply significant. Where was the dead man? The living water of life filled the open stone and coffin, and the eternal resurrection was portrayed in the language of the ancients on the surface of the marble. Thus was the Gospel to be understood.

To be sure, this was a gospel which had little in common with that which he had previously learnt and taught. It derived by no means from the leaves and letters of a book, but rather came welling up through grass, plants and flowers from out of the earth, or floating down with the light from the centre of the sun. All nature seemed to be animated and eloquent. Formerly dead and mute, she became active, confiding, frank and communicative. Suddenly she seemed to be telling the young priest everything that she had hitherto concealed. He seemed to be her favourite, her chosen one, her son, whom she was initiating, like a mother, into the holy secrets of her love and motherhood. All the abysses of terror, all the anxieties of his startled soul, were no more. Nothing remained of the pitch-darkness, all the fears of the supposed assaults of hell. All nature radiated goodness and love, and Francesco, overflowing with goodness and love, was able to requite her with goodness and love.

Strange: as he laboriously clambered upwards through broom, dwarf-beech and blackberry vines, often slipping on sharp-edged stones, the spring morning invested him like a symphony of nature, as mighty as it was blissful, which spoke more of creating than of the creation. Openly was revealed the mystery of a creative labour that was for ever exempt from death. Whoso did not hear that symphony, so it seemed to the priest, deceived himself when he presumed to join the Psalmist in his songs of praise: "*jubilate Deo omnis terra*" or "*benedicte cœli domino*".*

In sated abundance the waterfall of Soana roared down into its narrow gorge. Its roar sounded full and boisterous. Its speech could not be ignored. Striking one's ear now more muffled, now more clearly, in eternal variation, over the land floated the voice of satiety. Avalanche-thunder broke loose from the gigantic shaded steep of Generoso, and by the time it had become audible to Francesco the avalanche itself, with noiseless streams of rolling snow, had already poured itself down into the bed of the Savaglia. Where was there anything in nature which was not caught in the transformation of life and was without a soul – anything in which an urgent will was not exerted? The Word, Scripture, song and impelling heart's blood were everywhere. Did not the sun lay a delicious warm hand on his back between the shoulders? Did not the leaves of the laurel and beech thickets swish and sway when he brushed them in passing? Did not the water well up everywhere and describe everywhere, babbling softly, the lines and loops of its flowing script? Did not he, Francesco Vela, and did not the fibrous roots of innumerable growths, large and small, read it, and was it not its secret which was revealed in innumerable blossoms and flower chalices? The priest's hands lifted a tiny stone, and he found it covered with reddish strands: here too a speaking, colouring, writing wonder-world, a creative form, which bore witness to the universal force revealed in the plastic creation – the plastic force of life.

And did not the voice of the birds bear witness too, uniting like a network of infinitely delicate, invisible threads above the hollows of the titanic rock valley? This audible network seemed to Francesco at times to turn into visible threads of a silvery brilliance, set gleaming by an inward and eloquent fire. Was it not the love and revealed happiness of nature, made concretely audible and visible? And was it not delicious to note how this weft, as often as it was blown or rent asunder, was ever again reunited as with hastily flying, indefatigable shuttles? Where were the little feathered weavers perching? One did not see them, save perhaps when some little bird silently and swiftly changed its place; the tiniest throats poured out this super-exultant, far-flung eloquence.

Everything swelled, everything throbbed within him as well as round about him, and Francesco could not find the place where death had its abode. He touched the trunk of a chestnut tree and felt how it was driving the nutrient sap up through itself. He drank in the air as if it were a living soul, and knew at the same time that it was this to which he owed the breathing and the thanksgiving of his own soul. And was it not this alone which made of his throat and tongue a speaking organ of the revelation? Francesco paused a moment before a swarming, busily active anthill. A tiny dormouse had been devoured by the mysterious little creatures almost down to its graceful skeleton. Did not the pretty little skeleton, and the dormouse submerged and almost disappeared in the warmth of the ant colony, speak of the indestructibility of life, and had not Nature in her creative urge or compulsion merely sought a new form? Once more the priest saw, this time not below but far above him, the brown ospreys of Sant'Agata. Their winged and feathered bodies bore through space in majestic rapture the miracle of the blood, the miracle of the beating heart. But who could fail to see that the changing curves of their flight described on the blue silk of the heavens a clear and unmistakable script, whose meaning and beauty had the closest connection with life and love? Francesco felt exactly as if the birds were inviting him to read. And if they wrote with the course of their flights, then the power to read was not denied them either. Francesco thought of the far-reaching sight that is bestowed upon these winged fishers – and he thought of the countless eyes of men, birds, mammals, insects and fish with which Nature beholds herself. With ever-deeper astonishment he recognized the eternal motherliness in her. She made provision that nothing in the province of the mother-of-all should remain unenjoyed or hidden to her children: they had been endowed by her not only with sight, hearing, smell, taste and touch, but Francesco felt that she had prepared for all the transformations through the aeons countless additional senses. What a mighty seeing, hearing, smelling, tasting and feeling was going on in the world! And a whitish cloud hung above the ospreys. It was like a radiant pleasure-tent. But this too, as one looked at it, lost its place and was altered, in the liveliest mutation.

They were deep and mystic forces that had pierced the cataracts on the eyes of Father Francesco. But as a foil to this experience was the unspeakably blissful circumstance that he saw four delicious hours before him, which were to include a fresh meeting with the poor, outlawed shepherd girl. This consciousness made him confident and rich, as if time so delightfully spent could never pass. Up yonder, yes – up yonder where the little chapel stood, above which the ospreys circled – there was awaiting him a happiness, he thought, which the angels might envy him. He climbed and climbed, and the blissfullest zeal winged his steps. What he was planning to do up yonder must surely cause a sort of transfiguration to descend upon him, and make him, in detached proximity to Heaven, almost the equal of the good, eternal Shepherd himself. "*Sursum corda! Sursum corda!*"* He kept uttering the Franciscan greeting to himself, while by his side walked St Agata, the martyr to whom the little chapel on the peak had been dedicated, and who had gone to her death by the hangman's hand as to a merry dance. And behind her and him, so it seemed to Francesco in his eager ascent, followed a train of holy women, all of whom were going to witness the miracle of love on the festive summit. Mary herself walked with deliciously flowing, ambrosial hair and lovely feet far before the priest and his procession of sainted women, so that under her glance, under her breath, under her feet, the earth might be covered for all of them with festal flowers. "*Invoco te! Invoco te!*" breathed Francesco to himself in ecstasy. "*Invoco te, nostra benigna Stella!*"*

Unwearied, the priest had arrived at the summit of the conical mountain, which was scarcely broader than the tiny house of God that stood there. It also supplied space for a narrow ledge and a cramped little forecourt, the middle of which was occupied by a young and still leafless chestnut tree. A fragment of the sky or of Mary's blue robe seemed to be strewn about the little chapel in the wilds, so widely had the blue gentians spread about the sanctuary. Or one might also have imagined that the tip of the mountain had simply been immersed in the azure of the sky.

The choirboy and the two Scarabotas were already there, and had made themselves comfortable under the chestnut tree. Francesco grew pale, for his eyes had searched in vain, though but hastily, for the young shepherdess. But he put on a stern countenance and opened the door of the chapel with a large rusty key, without giving any sign of the disappointment and the dismay and struggle in his soul. He entered the diminutive church, whereupon the choirboy made certain preparations behind the altar for the celebration of the mass. From a bottle he had brought, some holy water was poured into the dried-up font, into which the two Scarabotas were now to dip their hardened, sinful fingers. They sprinkled and crossed themselves, and dropped on their knees in timid awe close by the threshold.

Meanwhile, Francesco, driven by agitation, betook himself once more into the open, where, with a sudden profound and silent emotion, after walking about a little, he found the girl he sought, somewhat below the topmost platform, resting upon a starry sky of brilliant blue gentians. "Come in, I am waiting for you," called the priest. She rose with seeming indolence, and glanced at him quietly from under lowered lashes. At the same time she seemed to be smiling with a lovely gentleness that was caused, as a matter of fact, merely by the natural formation of her sweet mouth, the charming light of her blue eyes and the delicate dimples of the rounded cheeks.

At this moment the picture that Francesco had cherished in his soul was fatally renewed and perfected. He saw a childlike, innocent Madonna face, whose distracting charm was combined with a very slight but painful bitterness. The striking redness of the cheeks rested upon a white skin, not a brown one, from which the moist crimson of the lips shone out with the glow of a pomegranate. Every strain in the music of this childlike countenance was at once sweet and bitter, melancholy and gay. In her glance was a shy retreat and at the same time a tender challenge, unconscious, flower-like, innocent of the violence of animal passions. If the eyes seemed to hold within them the riddle and the fairy tale of the flower, the whole appearance of the girl resembled rather a beautiful ripe fruit. This face, as Francesco's inner eye saw with astonishment, still belonged to an utter child, as far as the soul found expression in it; only a certain swelling roundness, like that of the grape, suggested that she had overstepped the boundary of childhood and reached womanhood. Her hair, partly earth-coloured, partly crossed by lighter strands, was wound into a heavy coil about temples and brow. Some trace of a ripe, heavy, inwardly fermenting slumberousness seemed to pull the girl's lashes downwards, and gave to her eyes a certain moist, over-urgent tenderness. But the music of her countenance changed below her ivory neck into a different one, whose eternal notes express a different meaning. With her shoulders the woman in her began: a woman of a youthful yet mature stature that almost tended to chubbiness and did not seem to belong to the childlike head. The naked feet and strong tanned legs supported a fruitful plumpness that the priest thought was almost too heavy for them. The head possessed unconsciously, or at most faintly divined, the sensuously ardent mystery of its Isis-like body. But for that very reason Francesco realized that he was irretrievably and for ever at the mercy of that head and that irresistible body.

But whatever the youth perceived, realized and felt in the moment when he looked once more upon this creature of God, so heavily burdened with a heritage of sin, one could detect nothing of it in his looks. His lips merely quivered a little. "What is your name?" he asked simply. In a voice that seemed to Francesco like the cooing of a heavenly laughing dove, the shepherdess said that she was called Agata. "Can you read and write?" he asked. She answered, "No." "Do you know anything about the meaning of the holy office of the mass?" She looked at him and made no reply. Then he bade her enter the little church and betook himself into it ahead of her. Behind the altar the choirboy helped him into his vestments; Francesco placed the cap on his head, and the holy service was ready to begin: never had the young man felt himself so full of a solemn fervour as on this occasion.

It seemed to him that the all-bountiful God had only just appointed him to be his servant. The road of priestly consecration which he had trodden seemed to him no longer dry, empty, illusory, as if it had nothing in common with the truly divine. The divine hour, the holy season had begun within himself. The love of the Saviour was like a heavenly rain of fire in which he was standing, and through which all the love of his own spirit was suddenly liberated and kindled to flame. With infinite tenderness his heart expanded over the entire creation, and was united with all other creatures in the same rapturous pulse-beat. From this intoxication, which almost stupefied him, burst forth in redoubled power his feeling of compassion for all created things, his zeal for the divinely good, and it seemed to him that for the first time he had a full understanding of the holy Mother Church and her service. At this moment he wished to become her servant with a renewed and wholly different zeal.

And how the journey, the ascent to this summit, had revealed to him the mystery of the office he had questioned Agata about! Her silence, before which he had himself grown mute, meant to him, although he had not betrayed it, that she shared his knowledge through the revelation that had now been experienced by them both. Was not the eternal mother the epitome of all transmutation, and had he not lured to this superterrestrial summit these neglected, darkness-encompassed, groping, lost children of God, in order to display to them the miracle of the Transubstantiation of the Son, the eternal flesh and blood of the Godhead? Thus the young man stood and lifted the cup with streaming eyes full of joy. It seemed to him as if he himself were becoming God. In this newly experienced state of being a Chosen Vessel, a holy instrument, he felt himself growing with invisible organs into all the heavens, with a sense of bliss and supreme power that made him feel as if exalted to an infinite height above the swarming spawn of the churches and their priestlings. They would see him, they would lift their eyes to him in astounded reverence as he stood on the dizzy summit of his altar. For he was standing before the altar in quite another and higher sense than that in which the holder of Peter's keys, the Pope, does after his election. In convulsive ecstasy he held the cup of the Eucharist and the Transubstantiation – as a symbol of the eternally new self-birth of the entire creation in the body of Christ – out into the infinity of space, where it shone like a second and brighter sun. And while he stood there with the elevated sacrament, an eternity in his estimation – in reality two or three seconds – it seemed to him as if the sugarloaf of Sant'Agata were covered from top to bottom with listening angels, saints and apostles. But almost more glorious seemed to him a hollow drumbeat and a line of beautifully dressed women, who, linked together with garlands of flowers and clearly visible through the walls, danced around the little chapel. Behind them whirled in ecstatic frenzy the maenads of the sarcophagus, while the goat-footed satyrs danced and pranced, some of them bearing in merry procession Luchino Scarabota's wooden symbol of fruitfulness.

The descent to Soana brought to Francesco, as to one who has drained the cup of intoxication to its dregs, a meditative disenchantment. The Scarabota family had gone away after the mass: brother, sister and daughter had gratefully kissed the young priest's hand at parting.

As he descended farther and farther into the depths, he grew more and more suspicious of the state of mind in which he had celebrated the mass up yonder. The peak of Sant'Agata had surely been in former times a place of pagan worship, and what had taken hold of him up there, apparently with the rushing sound of the Holy Ghost, was perhaps the demoniacal work of that dethroned theocracy which Jesus Christ had deposed but whose pernicious power was still tolerated by the creator and ruler of the world. Arriving at Soana and his parsonage, the priest was wholly possessed by the consciousness of having committed a grievous sin, and his anxieties on this account became so severe that even before his noon meal he entered the church, which stood wall to wall with his dwelling, in order to commit himself in ardent prayers to the highest Mediator, and perhaps be cleansed by His grace.

In a feeling of pure helplessness he begged God not to deliver him over to the assaults of the demons. He felt very clearly, he confessed, how they were attacking his soul in all manner of ways, now shutting it up, now causing it to expand beyond its previous wholesome limits, transforming it in the most terrible fashion.

"I was a little garden, carefully tilled to Thy praise," Francesco said to God. "Now it is drowned in a flood which is rising and rising, perhaps through planetary influences, and on whose shoreless waters I float helplessly in a tiny skiff.

Formerly I knew my path exactly. It was the one which Thy Holy Church prescribes for her servants. Now I feel rather drifting than certain of my goal and my path. Give me," pleaded Francesco, "my former restraint and my assurance, and command the evil angels to cease from directing their dangerous assaults against Thy helpless servant. Lead, O lead us not into temptation. It was in Thy service that I ascended to those poor sinners; help me to find my way back into the strictly limited sphere of my holy duties."

Francesco's prayers had no longer their pristine clearness and conciseness. He prayed for things which were mutually exclusive. At times he himself fell into doubt as to whether the stream of passion which carried his prayers came from heaven or from some other source. That is to say, he did not exactly know whether he was not actually beseeching heaven for some boon from hell. The fact that he included the two Scarabotas in his prayer might have its source in Christian compassion and pastoral care, but was it the same thing when with a fervour that brought him to scalding tears he prayed for the deliverance of Agata?

To this question he could for the present give an affirmative answer, for the clear stirring of his most powerful instinct, which he had felt on seeing the girl again, had passed over into a dreamy enthusiasm for something infinitely pure. This transformation was the reason why Francesco did not perceive that that fruit of a mortal sin was coming to take the place of Mary the Mother of God, and was for his prayers and thoughts, one might say, the incarnation of the Madonna. On the first of May there began in the church of Soana, as everywhere, a special worship of Mary – the observance of which put to sleep still more effectually the watchfulness of the young priest. Regularly, every day, at about the hour of twilight, he delivered a little discourse, principally to the women and daughters of Soana, which had for its subject the virtues of the Blessed Virgin. Before and afterwards the nave of the church resounded with songs of praise in honour of Mary, which rang out through the open door into the springtime. And with the delicious old airs, so beautiful in both text and music, there mingled from without the cheerful chirping of sparrows and the sweet plaint of the nightingales in the damp gorges of the neighbourhood. At such moments Francesco, while apparently serving Mary, was wholly given over to the service of his idol.

Had the mothers and daughters of Soana dreamt that in the eyes of the priest they formed a congregation which he was inviting to the church day after day to the glorification of that hated child of sin, or in order to have himself wafted on the devout strains of the songs in honour of Mary to the tiny pasture clinging far and high upon the crags, he would surely have been stoned. As it was, it seemed as if the young pastor's piety increased every day before the wondering eyes of the entire parish. Little by little, old and young, rich and poor – in short, everybody from the Sindaco to the beggars, from the most faithful to the most indifferent churchgoer – was drawn into the May madness of Francesco Vela.

Even the long solitary walks which he now took were construed in the young saint's favour. And yet, they were only undertaken in the hope that on such an occasion chance might lead Agata across his path. For fearing to betray himself he had arranged that the next special service for the Scarabota family was to take place only after an interval of more than a week, which now seemed to him unendurable.

Nature was still speaking to him in that open manner of which he had first become aware on the road to Sant'Agata, on the height of the little sanctuary. Every grass blade, every flower, every tree, every vine and ivy leaf was a word in a speech that issued from the primeval source of all being, and that even in the deepest silence spoke with a Titan's voice. Never had any music so permeated his entire being and, as he thought, filled it with the Holy Ghost.

Francesco had sacrificed the deep, peaceful sleep of his nights. The mystic awakening which had befallen him seemed to have slain Death, so to speak, and to have banished its brother Sleep. Every one of these nights of creation, throbbing with the pulse of the life that welled up everywhere, became for Francesco's young body a time of sacred revelation, so that it sometimes seemed to him indeed as if he felt the last veil fall from the mystery of the Godhead. Often, when he passed from heated dreams, which were almost a waking state, into the wakefulness of his senses, when out yonder the waterfall of Soana roared twice as loudly as by day, when the moon was contending with the darkness of the mighty ravines and black cloud banks were darkening in gigantic surliness the highest peaks of Generoso, Francesco's body trembled with prayers, fervent as never before, almost as when a thirsty tree, whose tops are being watered by the spring rain, quivers in the wind. In this state he would wrestle with God, full of longing to be initiated into the sacred miracle of creation, as into the flaming core of life, into that holiest, innermost Something that issues from thence and permeates all living things. He would say, "From thence, O Thou, my Almighty God, radiates Thy brightest light – from this flaming core that streams out in ever-inexhaustible waves of fire is diffused all the rapture of existence and the secret of the intensest pleasure. Lay not a completed creation into my lap, O God, but make me a co-creator with Thee. Let me participate in Thy never-interrupted work of creation: for only thus, and not otherwise, can I also become a participant in Thy paradise." Unclothed, Francesco would walk about in his room with the window wide open, in order to cool the heat of his limbs and let the night air surge about his body. And then it would seem to him as if the black thunderstorm were riding upon the gigantic rock-ridge of Generoso as a monstrous bull rides upon a heifer – snorting rain from its nostrils, bellowing, shooting quivering flashes from darkly flaming eyes and performing with heaving flanks the procreative labour of fecundity.

Ideas like these were altogether pagan, and the priest knew it without being as yet disquieted by it. He had already become too deeply immersed in the universal lethargy of the surging forces of spring. The narcotic vapour which filled his being loosened the limits of his confined personality and allowed him to expand onto the universe. Everywhere gods were being born in the dead morning of nature, and the depths of Francesco's soul opened likewise and sent up images of things which lay buried in the abyss of millions of years.

One night, while in a half-waking state, he had an oppressive and in its way frightful dream, which plunged him into a dreadful devotion. He became as it were the witness of a mystery which breathed a terrible strangeness, and at the same time something like the consecration of a primitive, irresistible power. Hidden somewhere in the rocks of Monte Generoso there seemed to be monasteries from which dangerous ladders and little stairways led down the rocks into inaccessible caverns. Down these ladders were climbing in solemn train, one after the other, bearded young and aged men in brown cowls who, by the absorbed character of their movements, as also by the remote expression of their faces, made one shudder and seemed to be condemned to the performance of a terrible rite. These wild and almost gigantic figures were venerable in an alarming way. They came down erect and tall, with vast, unkempt bushy heads on which no line divided hair from beard. And these celebrants of a pitiless and bestial worship were followed by women who were only clothed, as in heavy golden or raven mantles, in the mighty billows of their hair. Whereas the yoke of that passion kept the silently descending dream-anchorites under its spell in rigid insensibility, there rested upon the women a humility, as upon sacrificial animals that are offering themselves to some terrible deity. In the eyes of the monks there was a silent, insensible frenzy, as if the poisonous sting of some rabid beast had wounded them and infused a madness into their blood, a furious outburst of which was to be expected. Upon the foreheads of the women, in their devoutly, piously lowered lashes, there was an exalted solemnity.

At last the anchorites of Generoso placed themselves singly, like living idols, in shallow niches of the rock wall, and there began a phallic worship as ugly as it was sublime. Horrible as it was – and Francesco shuddered to the depths of his soul – it was equally thrilling in its deadly gravity and its fearful sanctity. Huge owls ranged with piercing shrieks along the rock walls, amid the plunging of the waterfall and in the magic light of the moon, but the deafening cries of the great night birds were outdone by the heart-stopping, anguished shrieks of the priestesses as they died of the torments of ecstasy.

The day of the divine service for the poor outlawed mountain-herders had finally come round again. Even in the morning, when Francesco got up, it resembled no other among all those he had ever experienced. Thus in the life of every privileged man, days spring up unexpected and unbidden, like a blinding revelation. On this morning the young man had no desire to be either a saint or an archangel, or even a god. Nay, he was rather seized with a faint fear that saints, archangels and gods might be made his foes by envy: for on this morning he felt himself exalted above the saints, angels and gods. But on the summit of Sant'Agata a disappointment was awaiting him. His idol, who bore the name of the saint, had absented herself from the churchgoing. Questioned by the blanching priest, the coarse, beastly father only produced coarse, beastly sounds, whereas his wife – who was at the same time his sister – excused her daughter on grounds of household work. Thereupon the holy office was performed by Francesco in so listless a manner that at the end of the mass he did not rightly know whether it had already begun. Inwardly he experienced the torments of hell: indeed such states of mind as, in comparison with a real fall from heaven to hell, made of him a poor damned soul.

After he had dismissed at once both the ministrants and the two Scarabotas, he descended at random one side of the steep peak, still utterly disconcerted, without being conscious of any goal, still less of any danger. Again he heard the nuptial cries of the circling ospreys, but they sounded to him like mockery poured out upon him from the deceptively gleaming ether. In the rubble of a dry watercourse he slipped, panting and leaping, while he whimpered confused prayers and imprecations. He was tortured by jealousy. Although nothing had happened save that the sinner Agata had been detained by something or other on the Alp of Soana, it seemed a settled thing to the priest that she had a lover, and was spending the time stolen from church in his villainous arms. While her absence brought home to his consciousness all of a sudden the immensity of his dependence, he felt by turns fear, consternation and rage, the impulse to punish her and to beg her for deliverance from his distress – that is, for the return of his love. He had by no means put off the pride – the wildest and most unyielding of all – of the priest, and this pride had been injured to the utmost. For him the default of Agata was a threefold humiliation. The sinner had spurned the man as himself, as the servant of God and as the giver of the sacrament. The man, the priest and the saint writhed in convulsions of downtrodden vanity, and foamed at the mouth when he thought of the bestial fellow, herdsman or woodchopper, whom in the meantime she was probably preferring to him.

With torn and dusty cassock, flayed hands and scratched face, Francesco arrived after some hours of wild and aimless clambering up and down gorges through thickets of broom, across rushing mountain waters, at a part of Generoso where herd-bells greeted his ear. He was not in doubt for a moment as to the place he had thus reached. He looked down upon deserted Soana, upon his church, which was clearly to be seen in the bright sun, and recognized the throng that was now streaming in vain towards the sanctuary. Just at this moment he should have been donning his robes in the vestry. But he could much more easily have cast a rope around the sun and drawn it from the sky than have rent the invisible fetters that were drawing him forcibly towards the Alp.

The young pastor was on the point of regaining a certain awareness when a fragrant smoke, carried by the fresh mountain air, ascended into his nostrils. Involuntarily looking about him with a searching glance, he beheld not very far from him the seated figure of a man who seemed to be tending a little fire, beside which was steaming a tin vessel, probably filled with a *minestra*.*

The seated person did not see the priest, for he had his back turned to him. Hence the priest on his part could distinguish only a round, almost white, woolly head, and a strong brown neck, while shoulders and back were covered with a jacket that age, weather and wind had made earth-coloured, and that hung loosely on him. The peasant, herder or woodcutter, or whatever he might be, sat bending over the little fire, whose scarcely visible flames, depressed by the mountain breeze, sent out horizontal tongues of fire and flat gusts of smoke along the earth. He was evidently absorbed in some task – a piece of carving, as it soon turned out – and was silent like one whose immediate occupation has made him forget God and the world. After Francesco had been standing a considerable while, for some reason or other anxiously avoiding any movement, the man or boy by the fire began to whistle softly and, having once begun to make music, suddenly breathed out into the air from a melodious throat the fragments of a song.

Francesco's heart beat violently. It was not because he had climbed so furiously up and down the gorges, but for reasons which derived partly from the strangeness of his situation, partly from the peculiar impression which the proximity of the man by the fire produced in him. This brown neck, this curly, yellowish-white hair, the youthfully abundant physique which one divined beneath the shabby covering, the recognizably free and satisfied behaviour of the mountaineer – all this formed like a flash a connection in Francesco's soul, in which his morbid and undirected jealousy flared up still more torturingly than before.

Francesco walked up to the fire. He could not have successfully hidden anyway, and he was moreover attracted by an irresistible urge. At this, the mountaineer turned around, showed a face full of youth and strength the like of which the priest had never yet seen, sprang up and gazed at the approaching stranger.

It was now clear to Francesco that he had to do with a young herdsman, as the carving he was executing was a sling. He was watching the brown-and-black-spotted cattle which, visible here and there, but on the whole remote and hidden, were climbing about among boulders and brush, betrayed only by the tinkle of the bells which the bull and some of the cows wore on their necks. He was a Christian, and what else should he have been among all the mountain chapels and the images of the Madonna in this region? But he also seemed to be a very particularly devoted son of the Holy Church, for, recognizing at once the garb of the priest, he kissed Francesco's hand with timid fervour and humility.

In other respects, however, as the latter saw at once, he bore no resemblance to the other children of the parish. He was more powerfully and heavily built; his muscles had something athletic about them, and his eye seemed to have been taken from the blue lake far below and to be as far-sighted as that of the brown ospreys which were circling as ever high about Sant'Agata. His forehead was low, his lips thick and moist, his glance and smile of a blunt frankness. Secretiveness and hidden guilt, such as are peculiar to many a man of the South, were not to be detected in him. Of all these matters Francesco took account, eye to eye with the blond young Adam of Monte Generoso, and confessed to himself that he had never seen such a naturally handsome oaf in his life.

In order to conceal the true reason for his coming and to justify his presence, he made up the lie that he had given the sacrament to a dying person in a remote cabin and then had started home without his ministrants. In doing so he had lost his way, slipping and sliding, and now wished to be put on the right path, after he had rested a little. The herder believed this lie. With coarse laughter and showing his healthy rows of teeth, and yet with embarrassment, he listened to the priest's story and arranged a seat for him, throwing the jacket from his shoulders and spreading it out on the roadside by the fire. This bared his brown and shining shoulders, and indeed his entire body to the waist: it became evident he was wearing no shirt.

To begin a conversation with this child of nature involved considerable difficulties. It seemed embarrassing to him to be alone with the clergyman. Kneeling, he blew into the fire awhile, put twigs on it, now and then lifted the lid of the kettle and spoke a few words in an incomprehensible dialect – then, suddenly, he uttered a mighty shout, which echoed and re-echoed from the rock bastions of Generoso.

Scarcely had this echo died away when someone was heard approaching with loud shrieking and laughter. It was various voices, the voices of children, among which was to be distinguished the voice of a woman alternately laughing and calling for help. At the sound of this voice Francesco felt his arms and feet go numb, and at the same time it seemed to him as if a power were making itself known – which, compared with the one that had produced his natural existence, contained the true and veritable secret of life. Francesco was flaming like the burning bush of the Lord, but outwardly he gave no sign. While his soul was insensible for many seconds, he felt an unfamiliar deliverance and at the same time a captivity as sweet as it was hopeless.

In the meantime the muffled, laughing female cries for help had been nearing, until at the turn of a precipitous path a bucolic picture became visible, as innocent as it was certainly unusual. The very same spotted goat that had pestered the priest Francesco on his first visit to the mountain pasture was leading, snorting and rebellious, a little bacchantic procession, and, pursued by shouting children, was bearing astride on his back the only bacchante of the troop. The beautiful girl Francesco thought he was seeing for the first time was holding in a powerful grasp the twisted horns of the goat, but strongly drawing the neck of the animal with her as she leant backward, she was unable either to force it to stand still or to slide off its back. Some bit of fun, which she might perhaps have undertaken to please the children, had got the girl into this helpless situation, in which, not really sitting but touching the ground with her bare feet on either side of her unsuitable mount, she was less carried than walking, and yet could not get free of the unruly, fiery buck without falling. Her hair had come down, the straps of her coarse shirt had slipped from her shoulders, so that one delicious round area was visible, and the short skirts of the shepherdess, which never reached quite to her calf, were now still less adequate to cover her voluptuous knees.

It took some little time for the priest to become aware who the bacchante really was, and that in her he had before him the hungrily sought object of his tormenting desire. The shrieks of the girl, her laughter, her involuntary wild movements, her loosened and flying hair, the open mouth, the spasmodically heaving and panting breast, the whole semi-forced, yet deliberate foolhardiness of the boisterous ride, had outwardly changed her entirely. A rosy glow overspread her face, and mingled pleasure and fear with a bashfulness which found droll and pretty expression when one of her hands darted like a flash from the horn of the animal to the dangerously disarranged hem of her dress.

Francesco was spellbound and captivated by the picture, which seemed to have the power to transfix him. It seemed to him beautiful in a way which did not suggest to him the remotest resemblance to a witch's ride. On the other hand, his thoughts of antiquity were revived. He remembered the marble sarcophagus which stood on the village square of Soana, ever overflowing with clear mountain water, whose sculpture he had lately examined. Was it not as if that world of the wreath-crowned wine god, made of marble and yet so alive – the dancing satyrs, the panther-drawn triumphal chariot, the female flutists and bacchantes – had hidden itself in the stony wastes of Generoso, and as if suddenly one of the god-inspired women, cut off from the frenzied mountain-worship of the maenads, had surprised them by appearing in present-day life?

If Francesco had not recognized Agata at once, on the other hand the goat had immediately recognized the priest – wherefore he dragged straight up to him his vainly shrieking and resisting burden, and by setting his two cleft fore hooves without any ceremony in the priest's lap, brought about the final release of his rider, who slowly slid down off his back.

The moment the girl realized that a stranger was present and actually recognized this stranger as Francesco, her laughter and her gaiety came to a very sudden end, and her face, which till then had been beaming with pleasure, took on a half-defiant pallor.

"Why did you not come to church today?" Francesco asked, rising to his feet, in a tone and with an expression on his pale face which one must have interpreted as angry, although it had for its cause a very different commotion in his soul. Either because he wished to conceal this agitation, or out of embarrassment, even helplessness, or because the shepherd of souls in him was really bursting with indignation, his anger increased and was displayed in a manner that made the herder look up in disapproval, but that spread alternately the flush and pallor of consternation and shame over the face of the girl.

But while Francesco was speaking and chiding with words – words that flowed easily from his lips without his soul's needing to be in them – all was calm within him; and while the veins were swelling on his alabaster brow, he felt the rapture of a deliverance. The utmost poverty of life which he had just been feeling was transformed into wealth, his torturing hunger into satiety – the accursed, infernal world of a moment before was now dripping with the glory of paradise. And the ecstasy of his wrath kept growing as it was being poured out more and more powerfully. He had not forgotten the despairing state in which he had just been, but his soul was jubilant now, and he could not but bless it again and again. For that state had been the bridge leading to happiness. So far had Francesco already been drawn into the magic circle of love that the mere presence of the beloved object brought with it that enjoyment which benumbs one with happiness and which permits no thought of deprivation, however imminent.

With all this the young priest felt, and no longer concealed from himself, the extent of the change that had taken place in him. The true state of his being had been laid bare to him, as it were. The mad chase which he had just completed was not prescribed by the Church, as he well knew, and was outside the hallowed network of roads that were clearly and strictly delineated for his labours. For the first time not only his foot but his soul had strayed into the pathless void, and it seemed to him that he had reached the spot on which he now stood not so much as man, but rather as a falling stone, a falling drop, a leaf driven by the gale.

Each of his angry words taught Francesco that he was no longer master of himself, but on the contrary was being forced to seek and exercise power over Agata at any cost. He took possession of her with words. The more he humiliated her, the more loudly resounded within him the harps of bliss. Every pain which his censure inflicted on her aroused a delirium in him: a little more – if only the herder had not been present – and Francesco would have lost in this delirium the last vestige of his self-control, and, falling at the girl's feet, would have betrayed the true beating of his heart.

Agata had preserved to this day, although she had grown up in that ill-famed household, the innocent mind of a flower. Her blue eyes, which resembled the mountain gentian, had never been seen in the valley, or down by the lake, any more than the gentian itself. The circle of her experience was limited in the extreme. Yet, although the priest was for her not really a man at all, but rather a thing between God and man, a kind of strange sorcerer, she suddenly guessed, and manifested it by an astonished look, what Francesco wished to conceal.

The children had led the billy goat up over the rubble and away. The woodcutter had not felt comfortable in the presence of the priest. He took his pot from the fire and climbed with it very laboriously up to a comrade, supposedly, who was lowering bundles of brushwood with an interminable wire over a precipice into the depths below. At intervals one of these dark bundles would crawl with a scraping sound along the rocky bastions, looking not unlike a brown bear or the shadow of a giant bird. Moreover, it seemed to be flying, since the wire was not visible. When the herdsman had disappeared from sight with a yodel of such great power that it re-echoed from the battlements and ramparts of Monte Generoso, Agata, as if crushed with penitence, kissed the hem of the priest's garment and then his hand.

Francesco mechanically made the sign of the cross over the girl's head, so that his fingers touched her hair. But now a convulsive trembling went through his arm, as if something were trying with its utmost strength to keep something else under control. But the straining, resisting something was yet unable to prevent the blessing hand from slowly spreading out, bringing its palm nearer and nearer to the head of the penitent sinner, and suddenly resting firmly and fully upon it.

Francesco cast a cowardly glance about him. He was far from wishing to lie to himself at this point, or to use the duties of his holy office to justify the situation in which he was, yet there flowed from him all sorts of words about confession and confirmation. And his almost uncontrolled, straining passion was so fearful it could arouse horror and detestation in case of discovery that it too once more took cowardly refuge behind the mask of priesthood.

"You will come down to my school in Soana, Agata," said he. "There you will learn to read and write. I will teach you a morning and an evening prayer – also God's commandments, and how you can recognize and avoid the seven cardinal sins. Then you will confess to me every week."

But Francesco, who had torn himself free after these words and had gone down the mountain without looking around, resolved the next morning, after a painfully wakeful night, to go to confession himself. When he revealed, not without disingenuousness, his qualms of conscience to the snuff-taking arch-priest of the neighbouring mountain town, called Arogno, he was most readily absolved. It was obvious that the Devil was opposing the young priest's attempt to lead straying souls back into the bosom of the Church, especially since, for a man, woman was always the most immediate occasion for sinning. After Francesco had breakfasted with the *arciprete** in the parsonage, and after many a frank word had been uttered concerning the frequent conflict between secular and churchly interests, while the open window let in soft airs, sunlight and birdsongs, Francesco yielded to the delusion that he was carrying away an unburdened heart.

A part of this metamorphosis was due, no doubt, to some glasses of that heavy, deep-purple wine which the peasants of Arogno pressed from their grapes, and of which the priest had a few hogsheads. Down into the vaulted cellar under huge, tender-leaved chestnut trees, where these riches were stored on crossbeams, the priest, at the completion of their meal, escorted his fellow priest and confessant. It was his habit to take down his flask at this time and fill it according to the needs of the day.

But scarcely had Francesco said farewell to his father-confessor on the flowery, wind-swept meadow before the iron-bound portal of the vaulted cave in the rock, scarcely had he stridden vigorously away around a turn in the road and put sufficiently hilly country, with tree and thicket, between himself and the other, than he began to feel an inexplicable repugnance to the consolation of his colleague and to the entire time that he had spent with him.

This dirty peasant – whose worn cassock and sweat-filled underwear emitted a repulsive odour, whose scurfy head and coarse hands, covered with ingrained filth, proved that soap was an alien thing to him – seemed to him rather an animal, or a clod, than a minister of God. The clergy are consecrated persons, he told himself – so the Church teaches – who have been endowed through the taking of vows with supernatural dignity and power, so that even angels bow down before them. This man could only be designated as a travesty on all such things. What a disgrace to see the priestly supremacy placed in such clownish hands – since even God is actually subject to such supremacy and is irresistibly forced by the words "*Hoc est enim meum corpus*"* to descend upon the altar in the mass.

Francesco hated him, yes, despised him. Then again he felt deep regret. At last it seemed to him as if the stinking, ugly, obscene Satan had chosen him for a disguise. And he thought of those creatures that have come to birth with the aid of an incubus or a succubus.

Francesco was astonished at these stirrings of his soul and at the course of his thoughts. His host and confessor had hardly given any occasion for it, aside from his existence – for his words, even at table, had been instinct throughout with the spirit of propriety. But Francesco was already floating once more in such a state of sublimity, felt himself to be breathing such a heavenly purity, that to him, compared with this hallowed element, the commonplace seemed to be permanently bound by the chains of perdition.

The day had arrived on which Francesco was expecting in his parsonage for the first time the sinner from the Alp of Soana. He had enjoined upon her to use the bell-pull near the church, by which one could call him to the confessional. But it was already approaching midday and still the bell had not stirred; while he, becoming more and more absent-minded, was teaching in the schoolroom some half-grown boys and girls. The waterfall sent in its roar, now swelling, now diminishing, through the open window, and the priest's excitement grew as the sound increased. He was full of concern lest he should miss the tinkle of the bell. The children were perplexed by his restlessness, his absent-mindedness. Least of all did it escape the girls – whose earthly, as well as their heavenly, senses feasted rapturously on the young saint – that his mind was not on his business, and hence not on them either. Linked by a deep instinct with the stirrings of his youthful being, they even shared in the suspense which dominated it at the moment.

Shortly before the peal of the noon bell there arose a murmur of voices on the village square, which till now had lain quietly in the sunlight, its chestnut tops covered with the shoots of May-time. A crowd of people was approaching. The sound of calmer, seemingly protesting, male voices was to be heard, but an irresistible stream of women's words, cries, curses and protests all at once far outswelled them and drowned them, making them inaudible. Then an ominous stillness ensued. Suddenly there came to the ear of the priest dull sounds, the cause of which was at first incomprehensible. It was May-time, and yet it sounded as when in the autumn a chestnut tree, feeling the force of a gust of wind, shakes down tons of fruit at a time: the hard chestnuts burst as they fall like drumbeats on the ground.

Francesco leant out of the window.

He saw with horror what was taking place on the piazza. He was so frightened – indeed so filled with consternation – that he was brought to his senses only by the shrill, ear-piercing peal of the confessional bell, which was being pulled with desperate persistence. In an instant he ran into the church and out in front of the door, and snatched the confessant – it was Agata – away from the bell-pull and into the church. Then he stepped out before the portal.

So much was clear: the entrance of the outlawed girl into the village had been noticed, and the people had done what they usually did at such times. They had tried to drive her, with stones, as if she had been some wolf or mangy cur, away from the haunts of men. The children and mothers of children had assembled and chased the ostracized, cursed being, without letting the beautiful girl-figure disturb them at all in the assumption that their stone-throws were aimed at a dangerous animal – a monster that was spreading pestilence and destruction. At the same time Agata, certain of the priest's protection, had not let herself be swerved from her purpose. Thus the resolute girl, pursued and hunted, had arrived before the door of the church, which was even now struck by some stones thrown by childish hands.

The priest had no need of chiding words to bring his excited parishioners to their senses: they had scattered and fled as soon as they saw him.

In the church Francesco had motioned to the panting, silent fugitive to follow him into the parsonage. He too was excited, and so the two heard each other breathing fitfully. Upon a narrow little staircase of the parsonage, between whitewashed walls, stood the horrified but already somewhat reassured housekeeper, ready to receive the hunted creature. One could see that she was ready to help in any way that might be needed. Only at sight of the old woman did Agata seem to become aware of the humiliating character of her present state. Passing from laughter to anger and back from anger to laughter, she uttered violent imprecations and thus gave the priest his first opportunity to hear her voice, which seemed to him to ring out full, sonorous and heroic. She did not know why she was persecuted. She regarded the little town of Soana much as she would have regarded a nest of mud wasps or an anthill. Furious and indignant as she was, it did not enter her mind to reflect upon the cause of this dangerous malignance – for, after all, she had been familiar with this condition from childhood, and accepted it as natural. But one fights off wasps and ants, too. Though it be animals that attack us, we are brought by them to hatred, fury, despair, as the case may be, and unburden our hearts, again as the case may be, by threats, tears or evidences of the deepest contempt. Agata did the same thing, and while the housekeeper was now twitching into place her miserable rags, she herself was gathering up the astonishing profusion of her rust or ochre-coloured hair, which had come down during her swift run.

At this moment young Francesco suffered as never before under the strain of his passion. The nearness of the woman who had ripened to maturity in the mountain wilds like a delicious wild fruit, the intoxicating glow which radiated from her heated body, the circumstance that the confinement of his own dwelling now embraced the hitherto distant and unattainable girl – all this brought him to such a pass that he had to clench his fists, tighten his muscles and set his teeth merely to remain upright in a condition that for a few moments completely clouded his mind. When it cleared again, he became aware of a monstrous turmoil of pictures, thoughts and feelings inside him: landscapes, people, the remotest recollections, moments in the past of his family and his profession, together with images of the present. Fleeing from these, as it were, an inescapable future rose up sweet and terrible, to which he knew he was completely bound. Thoughts flitted across this tumult of images in his soul – innumerable, restless, but powerless. The conscious will, Francesco realized, was dethroned in his soul, and another was reigning which was not to be resisted. With a shudder the young man confessed to himself that he had unconditionally surrendered to it. This condition resembled an obsession. But when there came over him a fear of his unavoidable plunge into the crime of a mortal sin, then at the same time he would fain have bellowed in the most ungovernable joy. His hungry glance looked forth with a totally new, astonished satisfaction. And more: in this case, hunger was satisfaction; satisfaction was hunger. The blasphemous thought shot through his mind that here alone was his imperishable, divine food, with which the sacrament gives heavenly nourishment to faithful Christian souls. His emotions were idolatrous. He declared that his uncle in Ligornetto was a poor sculptor. And why had he not rather been a painter? Perhaps he himself could still become a painter. He thought of Bernardino Luini* and his great painting in the old church of the monastery at nearby Lugano, and of the delightful blonde holy women that his brush had created there. But of course they were nothing compared with this hot, most living reality.

Francesco did not know at first what to do. A presentiment prompted him to flee, for the present, the proximity of the girl. All sorts of reasons – not all equally pure – urged him to seek out the Sindaco at once and acquaint him with what had happened before others could do so. The Sindaco listened to him quietly – Francesco had fortunately found him at home – and accepted the priest's point of view in the matter. It was but Christian-like, and the role of a good Catholic, not simply to overlook the deplorable conditions on the Alp, but to take an interest in the ill-famed family, ensnared in sin and shame. But as to the villagers and their conduct, he promised to take stern measures against them.

When the young priest had gone, the pretty wife of the Sindaco, who had a quiet, silent way of observing things, remarked:

"This young priest might easily get to be a cardinal – yes, even a pope. It seems to me that he is wearing himself out with fasting, prayers and night watches. But the Devil is always pursuing just the holiest ones with his hellish arts and with the most deceptive tricks and wiles. May the young man, with God's aid, ever be preserved from them."

Many desirous and many evil feminine eyes followed Francesco as he walked back to the parsonage at a pace as sedate as possible. They knew where he had been, and were resolved to use every effort to keep this pestilence of Soana from being forced upon them. Erect girls walking along with loads of wood on their heads, who had met him on the square near the marble sarcophagus, had, to be sure, saluted him with submissive smiles, but subsequently exchanged looks of contempt. As in a fever Francesco strode along. He heard the mingled warbling of the birds, the swelling and diminishing roar of the eternal waterfall, but it seemed to him as if his feet were not on the ground, but were being dragged forwards without a rudder into a maelstrom of sounds and images. Suddenly he found himself in the sacristy of his church, then in the nave before the high altar, as he prayed to the Virgin Mary on his knees for help in the turmoil of his soul.

But his prayers were not meant to have the effect of freeing him from Agata. Such a wish would have found no nourishment in his heart. They were rather a plea for mercy. The Mother of God should understand, forgive – perhaps approve. Abruptly Francesco interrupted his prayer and tore himself away from the altar as the thought happened to flit into his consciousness that Agata might have gone away. However, he found the girl still there, and Petronilla was keeping her company.

"I have settled everything," said Francesco. "The road to the church and the priest is free to all. Trust in me, what happened today will not be repeated." There came upon him such a resoluteness and assurance that it was as if he were once more standing on the right path and on good ground. Petronilla was sent to the neighbouring parsonage with an important church document. The errand could unfortunately not be postponed; and incidentally the housekeeper was to inform the priest of this incident. "If you meet anybody," the young man remarked with emphasis, "say that Agata from the high Alp has come and is here with me in the parsonage, and that she is being instructed by me in the doctrines of our religion, our hallowed faith. Just let them come and try to prevent it, and they'll draw down upon their heads the punishment of eternal damnation. Just let them cause an uprising before the church to maltreat their fellow Christian. The stones will not strike her, but me. I shall myself escort her as soon as it grows dark, though it were up to the very Alp itself."

When the housekeeper had gone, a long silence ensued. The girl had laid her hands in her lap and was still sitting on the same chair, apparently rickety, which Petronilla had moved for her up against the whitewashed wall. There was still a quiver in Agata's eyes, and the injury she had suffered was reflected in flashes of indignation and secret rage, but her full-cheeked Madonna-like face had more and more taken on a helpless expression, until at last a silent, copious stream bathed her cheeks. Francesco, meanwhile, with his back to her, had been looking out of the open window. As he let his eyes rove over the gigantic mountain walls of the valley of Soana, from the ominous Alp down to the lake shore, while with the eternal murmur of the waterfall the singing of a single fading boyish voice came to him from the luxuriant vine-clad terraces, he could not but hesitate to think that he now really had in his hands the fulfilment of his all-too-human desires. Would Agata still be present when he turned around? And if she were present, what would happen when he turned? Must this moment not be decisive for his entire earthly existence – yes – and even beyond it? These questions and doubts led the priest to keep the position he had taken as long as possible, in order to judge or at least consult himself once more before the decision was made. It was a matter of seconds, not of minutes: yet in these seconds not only the whole history of his entanglement, from the first visit of Luchino Scarabota onwards, but his entire conscious life, became immediately present to him. In these seconds a whole tremendous vision of the Last Judgement, with Father, Son and Holy Ghost in the sky, spread out above the topmost ridge of Generoso and terrified him with the blare of trumpets. One foot upon Generoso, the other upon a summit across the lake, the scale in his left hand, the naked sword in his right, the Archangel Michael stood terrible and threatening, while the abominable Satan had descended with horns and claws behind the Alp of Soana. But wherever the priest turned his glance, there stood wringing her hands a black-robed, black-veiled woman, who was no other than his despairing mother.

Francesco shut his eyes and then pressed his hands against his temples. Then, as he slowly turned around, he looked for a long time with an expression of horror at the tear-stained face of the girl, whose purple lips were trembling with pain. Agata was startled. His face was distorted, as if the finger of death had touched it. Speechless, he staggered over to her. And with the groan of someone vanquished by an inescapable power, which was at the same time a wild, life-hungry moaning and groaning for mercy, he collapsed upon his knees before her and wrung his clasped hands in her face.

Francesco would perhaps not have succumbed to his passion in such a degree for too long, had not the villagers' crime against Agata mingled with it a vague, burning, humane compassion. He realized what this creature, endowed by God with the beauty of Aphrodite, must, without a protector, look forward to in her future life and in the world. He had been made her protector by the circumstances of the day – had perhaps saved her from being stoned to death. He had thereby gained a certain personal claim to her – a thought which was not clear to him, but yet influenced his actions; operating unconsciously, it cleared away all sorts of inhibitions, timidity and fearfulness. And in his spirit he saw no possibility of ever again withdrawing his hand from the outcast. He would stand by her side, even if the world and God stood on the other. Such reflections, such tides of emotion, unexpectedly united with the stream of passion, so that the latter overflowed its banks.

For the moment, however, his behaviour was not yet a betrayal of what is right, the result of a resolve to sin: it was only a state of weakness, of helplessness. Why he did what he was doing he could not have told. In truth he was really doing nothing – only something was happening to him. And Agata, who really should have been frightened now, was not frightened, but seemed to have forgotten that Francesco was a stranger to her and a priest. He seemed all at once to have become her brother. And while her weeping broke into sobbing, she not only permitted him, now likewise shaken by dry sobs, to embrace her as if to comfort her, but she lowered her tear-streaming face and hid it on his breast.

Now she had become a child and he her father, by virtue of his seeking to comfort her in her sorrow. But he had never felt the body of a woman so close to him, and his caresses and his tenderness were soon more than fatherly. To be sure, he felt clearly that in the sobbing woe of the girl there was something like a confession. He realized that she knew to what a hateful love she owed her existence, and was weeping over it with him in equal sorrow. Her distress, her pain, he was bearing with her. Thus their souls were united. But he soon lifted her sweet Madonna face to his own, clasping her around the neck and drawing her to him, while his right hand bent back her white brow; and when he had long feasted greedy looks on what he thus held imprisoned, with the fire of madness in his eye, he suddenly dropped like a hawk upon her hot, tear-salted mouth and remained indissolubly fused with it. After moments of earthly reckoning, eternities of dazzling bliss, Francesco suddenly tore himself away and stood firmly on both feet, with the taste of blood on his lips. "Come," said he, "you cannot go home alone without protection, and so I shall accompany you."

A changeable sky hung over the Alpine world as Francesco and Agata stole out of the parsonage. They turned into a field path on which they climbed down unseen from terrace to terrace between mulberry trees and through garlands of grape vines. Francesco knew very well what lay behind him and what Rubicon he had now crossed, but he could feel no regret. He was altered, sublimated, liberated. The night was sultry. In the plain of Lombardy, it seemed, thunderstorms were moving about: their distant flashes shot up in fan-shaped rays behind the giant silhouettes of the mountains. The fragrance of the immense lilac tree under the windows of the parsonage floated down from thence with the passing, seeping water of the branching brooks, mingled with warm and cold breezes. The two inebriated creatures did not speak. He supported her as often as they climbed down the wall in the darkness to a lower terrace, and would perhaps catch her in his arms, so that her heart beat on his, his thirsty mouth clung to hers. They did not really know where they were going, for from the depths of Savaglia's gorge no path led up the Alp. They were agreed on this, however: that they must avoid the ascent to it through the village. But it was not their intention to reach any out-lying, any distant, goal, but to enjoy to the full what they had achieved.

How full of dross, how dead and empty the world had been hitherto, and what a transformation it had undergone! How she had changed in the priest's eyes, and how he had changed in hers! Forgotten and of no account were all the things in his recollection that hitherto had meant everything to him. Father, mother, as well as his teachers, had all been left behind like vermin in the dust of the old, rejected world – whereas to him, the son of God, the new Adam, the cherub had reopened the gates of paradise. In this paradise, in which he was now taking his first enraptured steps, there was a supreme sense of timelessness. He no longer felt himself a man of any particular time or age. Equally timeless was the nocturnal world about him. And since the time of expulsion, the world of banishment and of original sin, now lay behind him outside the guarded gates of paradise, he no longer felt the slightest fear for it. Nobody out yonder could injure him. It was not in the power of his superiors – not in the power of the Pope himself – even to prevent his enjoyment of the least of the fruits of paradise, nor to take from him the least fragment of that gift of grace, that highest bliss, which had once for all been bestowed upon him. His superiors had become inferiors. They lived forgotten in a long-lost world of wailing and gnashing of teeth. Francesco was no longer Francesco: he had just been awakened by the breath of God as first man, as sole Adam, sole master of the Garden of Eden. There lived no other man besides him in the expanse of this sinless creation. Constellations making heavenly music trembled with ecstasy. Clouds lowed like greedily pasturing kine, purple fruits radiated streams of sweet rapture and delicious refreshment, tree trunks oozed fragrant resin, blossoms scattered precious spices – but all this depended upon Eve, whom God had placed among all these miracles as the fruit of fruits, the spice of spices, upon her who was herself His greatest miracle. All the fragrance of the spices, their finest essence, the Creator had put into the hair, skin and fruity flesh of her body: her form and substance had no equal. Her form and substance was God's secret. Her form moved of itself, and was equally delightful at rest or in motion. Her substance seemed to be made from what lily leaves and rose petals are formed of, but a matter of chaster coolness and of hotter fire, at once more delicate and more resistant. In this fruit there was a living, throbbing kernel – delightful, quivering pulses beat in it – and when one tasted of her she bestowed little by little all the more delicious, exquisite raptures, while her heavenly abundance lost nothing thereby.

And the most delightful thing in this creation, this regained paradise, one could easily deduce from how close the Creator was. God had neither finished His work here and left it alone, nor had He laid Himself to rest in it. On the contrary, the creating hand, the creating spirit, were not withdrawn: they remained creatively at work. And every one of all the parts and members of paradise was creative. Francesco-Adam, having only just issued from the potter's workshop, felt himself creatively active in every direction. With a rapture which was other-worldly he felt and saw Eve, the daughter of God. There was still clinging to her the love that had formed her, and the most delicious of all substances, which the Father had utilized for her body, still had that unearthly beauty which was not sullied by the smallest grain of earthly dust. But this creation too was still quivering, swelling and shining with the heavenly fire of active creative power, and burning to be fused with Adam. And Adam again was burning to unite with her and enter into a new perfection.

Agata and Francesco, Francesco and Agata – the priest, the son of a good family, and the outlawed, despised shepherd maid – they were the first human couple, as they clambered hand in hand by nocturnal byways down the mountain. They were seeking the deepest seclusion. Silent, their souls filled with an inexpressible astonishment, with a rapture that swelled both their breasts almost to bursting, they descended deeper and deeper into the sublime miracle of the cosmic hour.

They were moved. The blessing, the holy election, which they felt resting upon them, mingled a serious solemnity with their infinite happiness. They had felt their bodies, had been united in a kiss, but they felt the unknown destiny to which they were going. It was the ultimate mystery. It was the very reason why God was creating, and why he had put death into the world, taking death into the bargain, as it were.

So the first human couple arrived at the bottom of the narrow gorge which the little Savaglia had worn. It was very deep, and only a faint, unfrequented footpath led along the brink of the watercourse up to the reservoir into which the mountain water plunged down from a dizzy height over a rock ledge. At a considerable distance from this point the brook was divided into two branches, which soon reunited by a small green islet which Francesco loved and had often visited, because it was made very lovely by some young apple trees that had taken root there. And Adam took off his shoes and carried his Eve over to it. "Come, or I die," he said more than once to Agata. And they trampled down narcissus and Easter lilies with the heavy, almost drunken tread of lovers.

Even here in the gorge there was summer heat, though the rushing flow of the brook brought coolness with it. How short was the time that had elapsed since the turning point in the life of that couple, and how far away everything had receded that lay before that turning point! Since the islet was rather remote from the village, the peasant who owned it, in order to be somewhat protected against the contingencies of the weather, had constructed – with stones, branches and earth – a hut which afforded a tolerably rainproof couch of leaves. It was perhaps this hut that had been in his mind's eye when Adam took with Eve the downhill instead of the uphill path. The hut seemed prepared to receive the lovers. Secret hands here seemed to have been advised of the approaching festival of the secret incarnation, for there were clouds of light about the hut, clouds of sparks, fireflies, glow-worms, worlds, milky ways, which sometimes ascended in mighty sheaves, as if they were going to re-people empty universes. They swarmed and floated at such a height through the gorge that one could no longer distinguish the stars of heaven from them.

Although they were familiar with it, this spectacle, this silent magic, was nonetheless wonderful for Francesco and the sinful Agata, and their wonder at it checked them for a moment. Is this the spot, thought Francesco, which I have so often visited and surveyed with satisfaction, really without any presentiment of what it would one day mean to me? It seemed to me a place whither one might withdraw as a hermit from the woe of the world and, renouncing all, immerse oneself in the word of God. What it really is – an island in the river Euphrates or Tigris, the secret blissfullest spot in paradise – I could not see. And the mystic, flaring spark clouds, nuptial fires, sacrificial fires, or whatever they might be, lifted him completely from the earth. When he did not forget the world, he knew that it was lying powerless before the gates of the Garden of Eden like the seven-headed dragon, the seven-headed beast that came up out of the sea. What had he to do with them that worshipped the dragon? Let it blaspheme against the hut of God! Its slavering would not reach their retreat. Never had Francesco – never had he as a priest – felt so close to God, such a security in Him, such an obliviousness of his own personality, and gradually, in the rushing of the mountain brook, the mountains seemed to boom melodiously, the rock crags to peal like an organ, the stars to make music with myriads of golden harps. Choirs of angels shouted through infinite space; like tempests the harmonies came roaring down from above, and bells, bells, chimes of bells, wedding bells, small and large, deep and high, immense and delicate, diffused an oppressive, blissful solemnity throughout the universe. And so they sank, locked in each other's embrace, upon their leafy bed.

There is no moment that tarries, and even though one tries with anxious haste to hold fast those of the highest rapture, try as one will, one finds no way to hold them by. His whole life, Francesco felt, consisted of steps up to the summit of the mystery he was now living. Where should one breathe in future, if one could not hold it fast? How should one endure an existence like the damned if one were once more expelled from the ecstasies of this innermost heaven? In the midst of the superhuman inebriation of pleasure the young man felt with shooting pain the transitoriness of it – he felt, in the enjoyment of possession, the torment of loss. It seemed to him as if he were drinking a cup of delicious wine and quenching an equally delicious thirst, but the cup was never emptied, and yet the thirst was never quenched. Nor did the drinker wish his delicious thirst to be satiated, nor his cup to be emptied, yet he sipped at it with greedy frenzy, tormented because he could never get to the bottom.

Enveloped by the rushing of the brook, overflooded by it, encircled by dancing fireflies, the couple rested on the rustling leaves, while the stars twinkled in through the roof of the hut. Of all Agata's mysteries, which he had marvelled at like unattainable treasures, he had taken possession fearfully. He had plunged into her loosened hair; his lips clung to her lips. But immediately his eye was filled with envy of his mouth, which had robbed it of the sight of the sweet mouth of the girl. And ever more incomprehensible, glowing and benumbing welled up bliss from the mysteries of her young body. What he had never hoped to possess, when hot nights would tantalize him with it, was nothing compared to what he now possessed without stint or limit.

And while he was feasting, he would ever and again become incredulous. The excess of his consummation always tempted him afresh to assure himself insatiably of his ownership. For the first time in his life his fingers, his trembling hands and palms, his arms, his breast, his hips, touched a woman. And she was to him more than woman. He felt as if he had recovered something that had been lost or flung away, without which he had been a cripple, and with which he had now united to form a perfect whole. Had he ever been separated from these lips, this hair, these breasts and arms? It was a goddess, not a woman. And besides, it was nothing that existed by itself: he burrowed into the heart of the world, and with his ears pressed against her virginal breasts he listened with blissful shudders to the heartbeat of the world.

That stupor, that half-sleep came over the couple in which the raptures of exhaustion turn into the delights of conscious feeling and the delights of conscious feeling into the raptures of oblivious stupor – so that now Francesco went to sleep in the arms of the girl, now Agata went to sleep in his. How strangely and confidingly had the shy, wild girl submitted to the pressing caresses of the priest – how devotedly and happily she obeyed him! And when she went to sleep in his arms, it was with the contented smile with which the satiated nursling's eye closes in the arms and on the breast of its mother. But Francesco surveyed the slumberer with astonishment and love. Her relaxed body was shaken by sudden shudders. Sometimes the girl cried out in sleep. But always it was the same charming smile when she opened her languishing lids, and then the same utter abandonment. As often as the youth dozed off it seemed to him as if some power were gently, gently wresting from him the body which he held in his embrace and which he touched everywhere with his own. But every time there followed upon this brief wresting sensation, as he awoke, a feeling of the intensest, most gratefully realized sweetness – an indescribable dream with a blissful, conscious sensation of the sweetest reality.

This was it, the fruit of paradise, from the tree that stood in the middle of the garden. He held it in the embrace of his entire body. It was a fruit from the tree of life, not from the tree of the knowledge of good and evil, with which the snake had tempted Eve. No, it was that fruit which, once tasted, made one equal with God. In Francesco any desire for a higher or other bliss had died out. Not on earth and not in heaven were there raptures that were comparable with his. There was no king, no god, whom the young man, rioting in excess of feasting, would not have felt to be a starving beggar. His speech had broken down to a stammer, to a jerky panting. He sucked in the bewitching breath which streamed out between Agata's open lips. He kissed away the tears of ecstasy, hot on the lashes, hot on the cheeks of the girl. With closed eyes, only blinking from time to time, each found in the other his own joy, with eyes directed inwards, with ardent, prescient emotion. But all this was more than enjoyment: it was something which human speech is inadequate to express.

Francesco celebrated early mass punctually the next morning. His absence had not been noted by anybody, his return not even by Petronilla. The haste with which he had to cleanse himself, join the waiting ministrants in the sacristy and betake himself to the altar before the expectant little congregation prevented him from fully recovering his senses. This happened when he was once more in the parsonage, once more in his little room, where the housekeeper set the customary breakfast before him. But this recovery did not at once bring the clearness of sobriety. Rather did the old environment, the rising day, give to his past experience the appearance of something unreal, which faded like a dream of yesterday. But here was reality, after all. And although it was more fantastic, more incredible than any dream that Francesco had ever dreamt, yet he could not disavow it. His had been a dreadful fall, there could be no quibbling about that: the question was whether any recovery at all from this plunge, this descent into sin, was still possible. The plunge was so deep and from such a height that the priest could not but despair of it. Not only from an ecclesiastical, but also from a worldly point of view this terrible fall had no precedent. Francesco thought of the Sindaco, and how he had talked with him about the possibility of saving the outcasts of the Alp. Only now, in secret and in his deep humiliation, did he recognize the whole priestly arrogance, the whole overweening conceit, that had puffed him up at that time. He gritted his teeth for shame; he writhed with degradation, as it were, like a vain, unmasked deceiver in naked helplessness. Had he not just been a saint? Had not the women and virgins of Soana looked up to him almost with idolatry?

And had he not succeeded in lifting the religious spirit of the village to such an extent that attendance at mass and at church was actually becoming habitual with the men once more? Now he had become a traitor to God, a deceiver and betrayer of his parish, a betrayer of the Church, a betrayer of his family honour, a betrayer of himself – yes, even a betrayer of the despised, outcast, ill-famed and miserable Scarabotas, whom he had ensnared more than ever in perdition under the pretext of saving their souls!

Francesco thought of his mother. She was a proud, almost masculine woman who had shielded and led him as a child with firm hand, and whose unbending will had also prescribed the course of his future life. He knew that her severity towards him was nothing but flaming mother-love, and that the least cloud on the honour of her son could not but utterly wound her pride, that a serious dereliction on his part must inflict an incurable injury on the very heart of her life. Strange that in connection with her the actual events that had been recently and clearly experienced could not even be conceived. Francesco had fallen into the most revolting slime, into the uttermost obscenity of depravity. He had abandoned there his vows as a priest, his essence both as a Christian and the son of his mother – yes, even as a human being. The werewolf, that stinking demoniacal beast, would have been all that was left, in the opinion of his mother, in the opinion of all men whatsoever, in so far as they had any knowledge of the crime.

The young man started up from the chair and the breviary on the table, in which he had pretended to be absorbed. It had seemed to him as if a hail of stones were rattling against the house – not in the manner of the previous day, when they were trying to stone Agata, but with a hundredfold, thousandfold strength, as if the parsonage were to be razed or at least turned into a heap of rubble, and he buried under it as the squashed corpse of a poisonous toad. He had heard strange sounds, terrible shrieks, frantic shouts, and knew that among the frenzied ones who were unweariedly throwing stones were not only all the people of Soana, the Sindaco and his wife, but also Scarabota and his family, and in the very foreground his own mother.

After a few hours very different fantasies and very different emotions had already displaced the previous ones. Everything that had been born of his heart-searching, his horror at the deed, his contrition, now seemed never to have existed. A wholly unfamiliar distress, a burning thirst, was drying him up. His spirit groaned, as one who rolls with parched throat on the burning desert sand crying for water. The air seemed to be lacking those substances required for breathing. The parsonage became a cage to the priest: he strode between its walls with aching knees, as restless as a beast of prey, resolved, if he were not freed, to rush against the wall and shatter his skull against it, rather than continue in such an existence. "How is it possible to live as a dead man?" he asked himself, as he observed the villagers through the window. "How are they willing or able to breathe? How do they endure their miserable existence, since they do not know what I have enjoyed and am now deprived of?" And Francesco felt as if he was growing inside. He looked down upon popes, emperors, princes, bishops – in short, upon all men – as men look down upon ants. Even in his thirst, his misery, his deprivation, he did so. To be sure, he was no longer master of his life. A supreme spell had totally robbed him of his will and turned him, without Agata, into a completely lifeless victim of Eros, of the god who is older and mightier than Zeus and the other gods. He had read in the writings of the ancients about this sorcery and this god, and had despised both with a smile. Now he saw clearly that one is actually driven to think of an arrow-shot and a deep wound, with which in the opinion of the ancients the god poisoned the blood of his victims. This wound burned, bored, flamed, rankled and gnawed within him. He felt terrible piercing pains – till at nightfall, inwardly almost screaming with happiness, he set out for that same little island-universe which had united him with his beloved the day before, and where he had agreed upon a new meeting with her.

* * *

The mountain herdsman Ludovico, known to the inhabitants of the district as the "heretic of Soana", fell into silence when he had come to the place where his manuscript broke off. The visitor would have liked to hear the end of the narrative, but when he was frank enough to express this desire, his host informed him that the manuscript went no further. He was of the opinion that the story might well end here – indeed must do so. The visitor agreed with him.

What became of Agata and Francesco, of Francesco and Agata? Did the story remain a secret, or was it discovered? Did the lovers find lasting or temporary pleasure in each other? Did Francesco's mother learn of the affair? And finally, the listener wished to know whether the story was based on real events, or whether it was out-and-out fiction.

"I have already said," replied Ludovico, paling slightly, "that a real incident set me to scribbling." Thereupon he was silent for a long time. "About six years ago," he continued, "a priest was driven with sticks and stones – literally – from the altar and the church. At any rate, I was informed by so many people, when I returned from Argentina to Europe and came to this region, that I have no doubt that this really happened. Moreover, the incestuous Scarabotas, though not under that name, lived here on Monte Generoso. The name Agata is invented; I simply took it from the little chapel of Sant'Agata, over which you see the brown ospreys are still circling. But the Scarabotas, among other children of sin, did really have a grown daughter, and the priest was accused of illicit intercourse with her. They say he did not disavow the fact, nor did he show the slightest remorse, and they insist that the Pope excommunicated him for it. The Scarabotas had to leave the region. They are said – the parents, not the children – to have died of yellow fever in Rio."

The wine, together with the excitement produced in the listener by the place, the hour and the company, especially by the reading of the composition, combined with all sorts of mystic circumstances, made him still more persistent. He asked again as to the fate of Francesco and Agata. In regard to this the herder could say nothing. "They are merely said to have been for a long time the scandal of the district, in that they desecrated and profaned the solitary shrines that are scattered about everywhere and misused them as asylums for their infamous lust." At these words the recluse burst out into loud, wholly unaccountable and unrestrained laughter.

Thoughtful and strangely moved, the writer of these travel incidents set out for home. His diary contains descriptions of this descent which, however, he will not insert here. The so-called "blue hour" that comes when the sun has sunk below the horizon was, at any rate, especially beautiful on that day. One heard the roar of the waterfall of Soana. Just so had Francesco and Agata heard it roar. Or were they perhaps still hearing its sound, even at this very moment? Did not Scarabota's stone building over yonder? Did one not hear the voices of merry children, mingled with the bleating of goats and sheep, coming from over there? The wanderer's hand passed over his face as if trying to tear away a veil of bewilderment: had the little narrative which he had heard really grown like some tiny gentian on a meadow of this mountain world, or had this glorious, supremely gigantic mountain profile, this petrified battle of giants, issued from the frame of the little story? This and similar other things he was thinking when his ear was touched by the sonorous voice of a singing woman. It was said, he remembered, that the recluse was married. The voice carried as in some spacious hall with fine acoustic properties, when people hold their breath merely to listen. Nature too held her breath. The voice seemed to come out of the rock wall – at times at least it seemed to stream out of the rock, in wide swoops full of fiery sublimity and the most melting sweetness. But it turned out that the singer was ascending from quite the opposite direction up the path to Ludovico's square hut. She was carrying a vase on her head, held slightly by her raised left hand, while she led her little daughter with her right hand. This gave the full and yet slender figure that straight, delightful bearing which makes such a solemn, even sublime impression. At the sight a sort of conjecture flashed like a revelation through the soul of the observer.

In all probability he had now been discovered, for the song suddenly ceased. He saw the climber approaching, with the full blaze of the western sky falling upon her. He heard the child – the mother answering with a calm, deep voice. Then he heard how the bare soles of the woman stepped with a slap on the rough-hewn steps. With such a burden one must step out firmly and confidently. For the waiting man the moments before this meeting were of unparalleled suspense and mystery. The woman's figure now appeared bigger. One saw the tucked-up dress, saw at every step a knee momentarily bared, saw bare arms and shoulders stand out, saw a round, womanly and – despite an air of proud self-consciousness – lovely face, surrounded in primitive fashion, as if by red-brown earth, with an abundant growth of hair. Was she not the man-woman, the masculine female, the Syrian goddess, the sinner who fell out with God in order to give herself wholly to man, to her husband?

The returning wanderer had stepped aside, and the shining vase-bearer walked past him, her burden allowing only a scarcely perceptible return of his salutation. She turned both eyes towards him, while her head continued to face straight forward. And over her face, as she did so, stole a proud, self-conscious, knowing smile. Then she again lowered her eyes to the path, while at the same time a superhuman light seemed to sparkle through her lashes. The observer was perhaps overheated by the warmth of the day, the wine and everything else that he had experienced, but this is certain: before this woman he felt himself grow quite, quite small. These full lips, curled almost in scorn for all their infatuating sweetness, knew that there was no contradicting them. There was no protection, no armour against the demands of that neck, those shoulders and that breast, blessed and stirred by the breath of life. She climbed up out of the depths of the world and past the wondering scribe – and she climbs and climbs into eternity as the one into whose merciless hands heaven and hell have been delivered.

Notes

p. 6, *Stracchino di Lecco*: A cow's-milk cheese from Lecco, in northern Italy.

p. 7, *Angelus*: A bell rung to mark the Angelus devotion – usually in three sets of three rings.

p. 13, *the greatest sculptor... there, too*: The reference is to the Swiss-Italian sculptor Vincenzo Vela (1820–91).

p. 18, *Sindaco*: "Mayor" (Italian).

p. 20, *Tiepolo*: The Venetian painter Giambattista Tiepolo (1696–1770).

p. 38, *Priapus*: The Greek god of fertility, usually represented by a phallus.

p. 45, *the prescription of the prophet... sacred verities*: Possibly a reference to Daniel 4:11–12.

p. 47, *Peter's vessel... holding the corners*: See Acts 10:11–12.

p. 50, *corpus femininum*: "The female body" (Latin).

p. 50, *Jesus where he tells... cliffs*: See Matthew 18:12–14 and Luke 15:3–7.

p. 51, *buen retiro*: "Place of recreation" (Spanish), from the name of the famous palace built by Philip IV of Spain (1605–65) near Madrid.

p. 52, *Vasari... and others*: The references are to writers, poets and artists Giorgio Vasari (1511–74), Johann Joachim Winckelmann (1717–68), Michelangelo (1475–1564), Dante (c.1265–1321), Petrarch (1304–74), Torquato Tasso (1544–95) and Ludovico Ariosto (1474–1533).

p. 53, *Ghiberti*: Lorenzo Ghiberti (1378–1455) was an Italian goldsmith and sculptor.

p. 56, *Behemoth*: A demonic beast mentioned in Job 40:15–24.

p. 56, *Asmodeus... whoring*: For the devil Asmodeus, see the apocryphal Book of Tobit, chapters 3 to 8.

p. 59, *jubilate Deo omnis... domino*: Psalm 100, which corresponds to Psalm 99 in the Latin Vulgate, begins "*jubilate Deo omnis terra*", and is usually translated as "Sing praises to God, all the world". "*Benedicte cœli domino*" is a reference to the Benedicite, a Catholic canticle – the second line of which, "*Benedicite, cœli, Domino, benedicite, angeli Domini, Domino*" is translated in the Book of Common Prayer as "O ye angels of the Lord, bless ye the Lord: praise him, and magnify him for ever".

p. 62, *Sursum corda!*: "Lift up your hearts!" (Latin). The expression is used at the beginning of the Eucharistic Prayer.

p. 63, *Invoco te... Stella!*": "I beg you... I beg you, our propitious Star" (Latin).

p. 76, *minestra*: An vegetable soup.

p. 85, *arciprete*: "Arch-priest" (Italian).

p. 86, *Hoc est enim meum corpus*: These words, which mean "This is my body" (Latin), form part of the Eucharistic Prayer. See Luke 22:19–20.

p. 90, *Bernardino Luini*: Bernardino Luini (*c.*1480–1532) was an Italian Renaissance painter.

CALDER PUBLICATIONS
EDGY TITLES FROM A LEGENDARY LIST

*Heliogabalus,
or The Anarchist Crowned*
Antonin Artaud

Babel
Alan Burns

Buster
Alan Burns

Celebrations
Alan Burns

Dreamerika!
Alan Burns

Europe after the Rain
Alan Burns

Changing Track
Michel Butor

Moderato Cantabile
Marguerite Duras

www.calderpublications.com

The Garden Square
Marguerite Duras

Selected Poems
Paul Éluard

*The Blind Owl
and Other Stories*
Sadeq Hedayat

The Bérenger Plays
Eugène Ionesco

Six Plays
Luigi Pirandello

Eclipse: Concrete Poems
Alan Riddell

A Regicide
Alain Robbe-Grillet

In the Labyrinth
Alain Robbe-Grillet

Jealousy
Alain Robbe-Grillet

The Erasers
Alain Robbe-Grillet

www.calderpublications.com

The Voyeur
Alain Robbe-Grillet

Locus Solus
Raymond Roussel

Impressions of Africa
Raymond Roussel

Tropisms
Nathalie Sarraute

Politics and Literature
Jean-Paul Sartre

The Wall
Jean-Paul Sartre

The Flanders Road
Claude Simon

Cain's Book
Alexander Trocchi

Young Adam
Alexander Trocchi

*Seven Dada Manifestos
and Lampisteries*
Tristan Tzara

www.calderpublications.com